HOT AND OFF LIMITS

FIONA WHITMAN

CONTENTS

CHAPTER 1

ZOE

We should have said *I do* by now…

Instead, I'm trolling the streets of my old hometown, still in my wedding dress no less.

Probably should've clued in the man I was marrying today…

I drive down the quiet tree-lined street and arrive outside Mom's cottage, the home I grew up in. It seems small. Tiny. Dark.

Just shut off the engine and get it over with, Zoe.

My heart is beating like crazy. I don't think I can do this.

I'm so over the pain and torment of helping Christina out of trouble.

It's a constant battle. Yet, here I am *again*, falling for her sob story. But, hell, she said Mom is about to die for fuck's sake. I had no choice but to flee the altar for her bedside.

Truth is, I'm really not ready to get married.

And I know if I tell my fiancé, he'll just tell me everything's going to be ok. Eternal optimist. Original *Mr. Niceguy*. Calm amidst my storm.

Maybe he's right.

After all, what's wrong with comfort, security, and dependability…even if we don't exactly go at it like teenagers…or much at all…

I guess not everything has to be passion-fueled. Passion doesn't pay the bills.

Nausea rises, and my hands shake on the steering wheel.

How can I just waltz in there? Mom on her deathbed, me pretending I haven't just ghosted her for almost five years.

I didn't even include her in my wedding. Or any plans for that matter. Because leaving this town with a clean break seemed like the right thing to do at the time.

Seriously, I can't do this. Serves me right for being gone so long. If Christina hadn't driven me almost to my breaking point before leaving this god-forsaken town, I could have at least stayed in contact with Mom.

My foot presses the gas pedal and I continue past the house.

Shit. I can't drive the block all night. Gonna have to go back there sooner or later.

I need a drink. A strong one. Not that I'm an advocate for using substances to fix problems…that's my sister's specialty. But, boy, this *very* second, I need whiskey.

A couple more blocks and I'm in the main drag of Hillsdale. Don't blink, or you'll miss it.

I come up to the neon light of the only bar in town, Buddy's Bar & Grill. Wonder if old Mr. Grant still runs this place. Sure would be nice to see a friendly face. He always had kind words and a warm smile for his customers.

But who else will be there? I can't face answering questions or knowing they are gossiping about me while I'm in the same room.

At least the parking lot looks practically empty.

Damn. I can't go in looking like this. I'm in my fucking white wedding dress! I guess I can change, but getting out of this fitted dress is a little awkward.

I slow the car outside the bar. Still has the same old *Help Wanted* sign. Been there since his son left. All sorts of bad he turned out to be, rumor had it.

One thing I definitely remember - he was *way* hot. Not that my nineteen-year-old self knew what to do with a man like that.

Come to think of it, my twenty-nine self probably doesn't either.

I could dream though. And back in the day, I did a *lot* of dreaming about him.

Jacob Grant. Dark eyes, chiseled face, body of a god… way, way too much of a maverick and probably a dozen years older than me.

He was more in Christina's league. She was always a natural bad-boy magnet and I…well, I went in a different direction. I was always the shy sibling. Lame.

One time he'd looked at me with something that seemed like pity or amusement. My insides went to mush, and my face burned so hard. How damn embarrassing.

There are other memories too…

That ass for instance. Mmm.

Oh, what the hell? Stop sitting here, lusting over the past.

I need to see my dying mother, and not lose my shit with my impossible sister. Sooner or later, I had to go back to that old house I grew up in and see them.

Right. One quick drink and I'll go.

I shut off the engine and peer into the back seat. I spot my long hoodie jacket underneath my suitcase. Perfect.

Luckily, I chose a short, elegant wedding dress, not some big, flouncy style. Just some lace detail on the bodice and cap sleeves. The jacket should disguise it while I grab a quick drink.

I step out of the car and pull the soft knit jacket around me. Feels like an old friend.

I'm tempted to pull the hood low over my head. But I'd probably just get harassed for trying to rob the place.

Chances are, I won't know anyone but old Mr. Grant anyway.

Then another thought. Shit, will anyone think I'm my sister?

Just breathe. Okay, girl, you got this.

After all, walking into the local bar has got nothing on facing my dying mother and the guilt of leaving her when she needed me most.

Christina…how could you sink so low, to not let me spend the last years with Mom? So selfish. The real question is, why am I even surprised?

I push the bar door open and quickly glance around.

A knot of anxiety. My feet are like lead blocks. Thankfully, it's pretty empty. Sundays might be like that here.

Doing my best to keep it together. Just wish the nerves would stop cartwheeling in my belly.

I look at the bar. Hm. No bartender. Stupid idea. I should leave. I don't need whiskey to solve my problems.

"Babe!" The sting of a heavy hand slapping my ass cheek. Without thinking, I swing around and smash a slap across his cheek.

"Fuck. You bitch! I should teach you some manners..."

This beast is up in my face, his sour breath assaulting my nostrils.

"Back off, asshole." I play it tough, but on the inside, I want to run and cower.

The stinky ape touches my face. "C'mon Christina. You're always friendly. C'mon babe…you like it when I grab you."

I'm about to drive my knee into his groin when a deep, gruff voice stops me.

"Get away from her. That's not Christina. Fuck, Bear! Leave her alone!"

A mountain of a man rips the drunk off me. He shakes him by the shoulders like he's the weight of a feather.

"Go home before you get me closed down."

"I'm not that drunk. I can see it's Christina." Stinky ape looks at me with wide, glassy eyes.

"It's her twin sister, you animal. Get out before I ban you."

"Twins? That might be fun."

"Bear, fuck off now. I don't want to drag you out, but I will." His voice, little more than a wild growl, penetrates my soul.

"Relax. Just a joke. Calm down." Bear shuffles away.

"Wait Bear…you okay to get home?"

"Yeah, man. I'll walk. Not far. Sorry lady who isn't Christina."

The mountain man makes a giant fist and thumps the bar. "Everyone, finish up. Bar's closed."

A collective groan erupts from the few remaining patrons. I can't blame them, it's barely evening. Does everything close so early here?

Apparently so, because they finish their drinks and file out.

He nods towards a newly vacant bar stool. "Take a minute. You need it."

As I sit down, it hits me. This man knows I'm not my sister. I don't remember knowing anyone this tall and broad from this town, or anywhere ever.

He locks the door and lopes back behind the bar. "Fuck me…last thing I need is a lawsuit. I should've cut him off an hour ago. Sorry. You okay?"

I nod. His dark gaze unsettles me, and my body tingles. It can't be…he was half the size and beardless last time I saw him. Wow, now I really need whiskey.

Like he's reading my mind, two shot glasses hit the bar, and he pours a nip into each.

"On the house." He downs one at lightning speed and nudges the other toward me.

"Go on. Settle the nerves. Long time, no see."

His friendly grin lights my insides and I feel my face warm again.

"Jacob?"

He nods. "Zoe, right?"

His long-lashed, dark-brown eyes study me again. I take the glass and down the contents. Ah, yes. Nothing like the burn of a great whiskey.

I push the glass back toward him just as he reaches for it, and a zap of electricity snaps at our touch. I giggle. Whoa, nineteen again…

Zoe Olsen doesn't giggle anymore. What am I doing? Pull it together, *right now*.

"You left suddenly." Oh great Zoe, just go right for the elephant in the room.

"Yeah," Jacob looks at me carefully, "and I wasn't hauled off to jail like the rumors said…But I was sure headed that way, so I joined the Navy, and was recruited into Seals."

"You still doing that?"

"Nope. Two tours of duty then went solo as a bounty hunter. Out of it all now." He runs his hand over his short beard.

"At least you had some excitement. I was a bank teller, and most recently, accountant." Honestly, Zoe, can you sound more boring? Sigh.

I look around the bar. "I was expecting to see Buddy here."

"He passed away a few weeks ago."

"Oh, I am so sorry, Jacob. He was a very kind man. Had so much warmth."

"Yeah, it was sudden, and he didn't suffer. Thank god for that."

His eyes study me again. "You look good, Zoe. Older."

Older? What the fuck? "Looking a little ancient yourself." I can't help but smile. He looks completely embarrassed. I kinda like that.

"Ah, maybe more mature than when you saw me last." He shakes his head and pours again. "You're even sexier than I imagined you'd be."

I choke on my drink. Was he drunk? "I think you're remembering Christina, not me."

He laughs, deep and raw. I could listen to that all night. "Oh, shit no. I know Christina and, *no*. Cool chick, but not my type."

Well, that's a rare comment.

He's still staring at me intently. I need to go, before I jump him right here on the bar. "Thanks for the hospitality. I gotta go."

"In town long?"

"Not if I can help it." I step down from the bar stool, and head for the door.

"Good luck with that. I said the same thing two months ago." Jacob edges in front of me to unlock the door. "Where are you off to now?"

His tone is suggestive.

I feel my pulse quicken. "Look, I've got a lot of personal shit draggin' on me right now. I'm not in the best headspace…"

He pulls the door open. Cool, welcome air. I feel my nipples tighten…and my desire heighten.

We stand in the doorway with Jacob looking down at me.

He licks his lips. My body surges.

"Maybe I can help you forget your troubles for a bit. No ties. Just some…release."

Our eyes lock.

Just get out of here. "I don't think so, Jacob."

I move toward the car, but can't resist one yearning look back.

He's in the doorway watching me, the broad cut of his shoulders and bulge of his biceps practically fills the space. I see his hand trail down his thigh and drag slowly back up.

Why should Christina get to make all the wrong decisions, and have all the fun? Just this once, I'll take what I want, and right now I never wanted anything like I want Jacob.

I run back to his waiting arms. He encloses me in a powerful embrace. Heaven.

Just a kiss, can't hurt.

He kisses the breath out of me with that sinfully attractive mouth. I let him kiss me again, and again until I can take no more without having sex right here in the doorway of the bar.

The dress I was meant to get married in rides up my thighs, along with Jacob's hand.

I groan as he presses me against the door frame. I feel his hardness and have no illusions about his size.

Throbbing for him now…I know I should stop…But the heat of him feels like it could cure all my problems.

His lips move down my throat, nibbling and licking. He groans, sounding as needy and desperate as I feel. Hot breath against my skin and his hand presses between my thighs. I throw my head back and let my breath out all in a rush.

I feel his mouth pressing against my ear. Rasping breath. "Zoe. I want you. I can't stop…"

"Jacob…I-"

Shit. *I'm in my wedding dress!* Lord, forgive me. I've left a man I don't love at the altar and my mother is dying, while I'm downing whiskey shots, and about to have sex.

"Wait!" I push him away. "I can't. I'm sorry. I should never have kissed you."

He rakes his hand through his hair. "Suit yourself," his voice raw, "your loss."

I run back to the car and get in. I'm so hot, I'm panting and rip off my jacket.

Pretty sure nothing could be as hard as dragging myself out of Jacob Grant's arms. One thing's certain. I need to leave this town as soon as I can. I can't deal with ever having to deny him again.

CHAPTER 2

JACOB

Zoe came back. Can't believe it.

Heat of the moment, I guess. Not complaining. Couldn't stop myself anyway.

But I'd never had a woman make me feel so out of control, ever. Her needy mouth and throaty moans had my jeans near bursting apart…wow! That sexual connection, as if we're matched for each other…Fuck, I'm going soft thinking things like that.

Fate and soulmate talk only ever got me hurt.

Reel it in, big boy. Not in any position to be jumping into complications like that. Even with Zoe Olsen. My hard heat twitches as I think of her soft lips. *That's enough outta you for one night.* Nothing but trouble.

We had an encounter, no big deal. Under different circumstances…No point dreaming about should haves or could haves.

Anyway, I can't afford any distractions right now. This was just about sex. She needed it. I sure as hell wanted it. We didn't have it. Nothing to see here, move along.

Don't expect to see her again.

Our conversation in the bar floats back into my brain. For an ex-bounty hunter, I sure sounded like a total jackass.

It was a shock to see her. I've never forgotten sweet Zoe. The one person I hoped was here when I came back. Even though relationships are a thing of the past for me, I wanted to see her again.

I asked Christina about her once. I never made that mistake again. Boy, could that lady get mad.

Must be getting fucking old. *And*, I called *her* old. What the hell is up with that? First, she nearly got accosted in my bar, then I told her she looks older…and then I hit on her when she tried to leave. *Idiot*.

Whatever possessed her to come back for a kiss, I don't know, but I bet she never makes that mistake again. No wonder she took off like the devil was on her tail.

Never liked taking no for an answer, but this time it hurts like a bitch. A knockback never killed anyone, so why do I feel like punching the goddamn fucking wall?

It's not like I'm hanging around Hillsdale for long anyway. Not like I want to start anything I can't finish. If I'm being honest though, I want to start something with Zoe.

Can't. My future is elsewhere.

I knew she wanted me. Once upon a time, I'd have taken the kiss, the girl, and the victory… and moved on. But those victories seem shallow now.

Bad timing. The only timing I know.

I have to let it go. Things always seem intense in the heat of the moment. Time for a reality pill.

Anyhow, as soon as everyone sees the *For Sale* sign in the morning, my ass will be toast in this town. They'll hate me.

But I'm not my dad, and I can't keep this place running to save all the lame ducks like he did.

I wanted to let Dad's friends have time to come to terms with his sudden passing, before banging a big-ass sign in the window. But it's long enough.

Dad is gone, and soon, I will be too. I replace the dusty *Help Wanted* sign for the *For Sale* sign. There. Done. Deal with it.

Time to get real and push forward with my decision. I'm going where no one can find me. For the sake of my sanity...and maybe my life.

My years as a bounty hunter didn't leave me unscathed. Not a day goes by, hell not an hour, when I'm not looking over my shoulder waiting for some old grudge to resurface for revenge.

I need to get my name off the licenses to this bar, so no one can trace me. And I have to get as far out of society as I can. How can I expect anyone to live like that, or to put up with my crazy nightmares? I haven't slept a night all the way through in years.

Pretty sure Zoe isn't interested in living off-grid. But I'd sure as hell like to get up in her grid again. I swig another whiskey down and shove the day's cash into a bag to throw in the safe.

Good thing she took off. Not in the market for a relationship. Not now, not ever. Save me the humiliation. Zoe deserves better anyway.

I don't have the capacity to love anyone again. Not after Bianca jilted me at the altar.

For all the gruesome stuff I've experienced, that day still ranks right up there.

It wasn't the first time she'd disappeared. She would often take off somewhere and not show up till days later. She always had some story…A dying grandmother- I think she had three, a long-lost cousin, or some old friend who needed her.

Once she told me she was on a twelve-day retreat with an Indian shaman…Then I got a call one night from my credit card company asking me to approve a transaction from a Vegas hotel.

I somehow knew it was her. She still denied it even though she drunk-dialed me at 4am that night. She wasn't in much of a coherent state.

Yep. The signs of her addictions and twisted mindset were obvious. But I didn't want to know. She was a trainwreck. Now that I think about it, probably our messed-up heads brought us together.

I was never tempted to take substances to forget. I didn't survive my junkie mom just to go down that soul-destroying route myself.

Buddy basically saved me twice. First from my messed-up birth parents by adopting me. And later by encouraging me into the disciplined world of the Navy. A strict routine, sense of purpose, and physical training became the recipe for keeping my head together.

When those habits waned, I met Bianca. Guess her woo-woo nonsense was right about one thing, you attract what you put out. My scrambled brain and her fragile mindset were definitely on a similar wavelength, for a while at least.

While I'm still majorly pissed and never want to see her again, I'm also relieved that I got a narrow escape. Her rejection eventually led me back to that survival recipe I learned in the Navy.

I still can't believe she called me last week. I never answer an unknown number. But It could have been a potential buyer. They're scarce animals these days. The bar's been listed online for three weeks with no interest.

As soon as I heard her voice, I should have blocked her lying ass. But I was stunned…how the fuck did she get my number anyway?

"I'm sorry, Jacob. I just got cold feet." Her pleading words had left me unmoved.

I was done with her excuses. Didn't even feel hate anymore…despite two years of bullshit. Two wasted years of me believing I was cut out to be a husband. A soulmate. Meant to be. Fated. *Fuck off.*

"I don't want to hear it, Bianca." I'd been tempted to reach for the whiskey bottle right there and then.

"I was wrong. We were good together, baby. I should've married you that day." Her whiny voice sounded desperate. How did I ever think I was in love with her and her warped neediness?

"C'mon Jacob, can't we meet? Say you'll forgive me… I'll make it up to you. Remember the good times baby? We can be all that again…"

That really pissed me off. "It's been months now. I'm over it. Over you. I'm glad you left me at the altar. I dodged a bullet. You did me a favor. Thank you."

"I'm going to prove to you that we're meant to be together."

"Stay away from me Bianca." I'd finally had the sense to terminate the call.

Any woman who can do that to a man, just not show up at your own wedding, has no heart. Even with her addictions, she must have known way before the actual day that something was up. Why can't people just be honest?

Just say, *I don't think this will work out*. Say, *oh sorry, I'm calling the wedding off.* Say, *I'm out*. I don't know, say any damn thing before a man is standing there in front of fucking everyone, waiting for his soul mate to appear and pledge her undying love forever.

Definitely, do not run off with another navy guy who is supposed to be the friend of the man you are damaging beyond repair.

Right there, the number one reason I'm never getting romantically involved again. Ever. And why I'll never accept dishonesty from someone I should be able to trust.

Time to go back to not caring about feelings, about anything. Dad's gone. No other family. Can't rely on family to care for you anyhow.

Why the fuck can't I have a normal life like everyone else?

My life was never normal. And when I last knew Zoe, she was only around nineteen, and way too nice for some much older punk who thought he knew everything. I was invincible. And all my buddies had already landed in jail or been arrested at least once.

That's when Dad begged me to straighten up before it was too late. For once, I decided to listen.

Now it's time I listen to my own good advice. Feelings get you nowhere. Stick to the plan.

For sure, Zoe could not be part of the plan. I guess it's better that she stopped us. Dodged another massive bullet. Lucky me. Lucky, lucky me.

So, if you are up there listening, God, or whoever…just keep Zoe out of my bar. Get Zoe to leave town ASAP and I'll behave myself…

Who am I kidding?

Shit, now she's got me talking to myself. I need a bed. Uh, there it goes again, swelling from my loins.

CHAPTER 3

ZOE

Don't think twice, Zoe. Shut the engine off, and get out. Not sure if it's the whiskey, or the need to get this done and get away from here, but I'm ready to face whatever's waiting.

I need to get my life together and forget that slice of heaven, Jacob Grant.

And, stay calm...

Christina appears, her red hair shining brightly under the porch light. She doesn't waste a beat, glaring daggers as she rushes down the steps.

Here we go…*drama central.* At least I'm not bailing her out of jail this time. Or scrambling to prove I'm *me*, the stable one…and not *her*, the hot mess. That I wasn't the one who'd recklessly stolen, damaged, or destroyed whatever stood in her selfish, morally deficient path.

"Can't believe you're back. Thought you'd chickened out when I saw you drive off an hour ago."

"Whatever," I look into her face, and our shared features

confront me, "you could've told me sooner Mom is so sick."

"You could've stayed in touch. But you were too busy pretending we don't exist."

"That's crap." If only she knew what just happened…I'm light years from perfect.

"Really? Then your fiancé, sorry *ex-fiancé*, knows you have a mother and twin sister living in Hillsdale?"

I stay silent. We're identical. Physically. But we're *nothing* alike where it matters.

"Exactly. You can pretend we don't exist all you want, but that doesn't make it true."

"Oh, believe me, I know." I spit out vengefully, "as much as I'd often like you not to exist, and avoid all the hurt you've caused me with your lies and scams, you always show up again needing something."

"Well, you might be surprised. A lot has changed in five years." Christina's flashing green eyes are as intense as the inner turmoil I'm feeling.

Christina was always changing, starting her life afresh. Kicking the habits. Cleaning up her act.

"I doubt it." Not falling for those lines again. "I'm just here to see Mom, not listen to your fake promises."

I start gathering my things from the back of the car. But she's not done.

"*Sorry*, I keep forgetting you were born perfect, *so* much better than the rest of us."

"I'm nothing like you, Christina, that's for sure. How did you get my number anyway? One of your thug boyfriend's investigate me?"

"You know Zoe, it's so nice of you to call your family and share your *special* day." Christina's sarcastic laugh cuts through my exhausted brain.

"And how did you know I was supposed to get married today?"

"Ha. Can't keep secrets from your identical twin forever. We're connected. Two peas in a pod."

That irritating, smart-ass laugh again.

"I'm nothing like you…"

"Oh no, not at all, we only share looks and DNA you dummy. Quite handy for me, helped me out of plenty of scrapes."

"I'm just here to see Mom."

God, I can't concentrate. I'll get my stuff from the car later. It's getting late and I need to see Mom.

And still, she goes on…

"Deep down, you're just the same as me. You know it, and I know it. DNA doesn't lie. You're just better at hiding it than I am. I know where I come from, and what you see is what you get."

I'm fighting back tears now. What if she's right? It's my greatest fear, that I'm more like her than I want to admit.

Look what I've done. Left the man I'm supposed to marry, and almost had sex with another man…in my wedding dress! What the hell was I thinking?

Still, I deny it.

"We're nothing alike, Christina. You've made my life a misery, and I can't wait until you're out of it again."

I step up the front porch steps. Doubt this part will go well either.

"Time you got brought down a peg or two. See what the real world is like!" Christina yells from behind me.

Deep breaths, Zoe. Ignore her. Just stay one night, hold your peace, and let it go.

I enter the dimly lit house. The house's eerie familiarity wraps around me.

I'm relieved everything looks clean and tidy, apart from some colored pens and books scattered all over the dining table.

I nervously prepare myself for seeing Mom…sick and bedridden.

I hear the television in her bedroom and look inside. She lets out a loud laugh and claps her hands.

There she is…sitting in a chair, watching some reality show, and…vaping? Death bed? I'd never seen her look so vibrant. Our eyes meet, and she drops her vape.

"Zoe!"

My dry mouth won't utter a single sound.

"Well, come sit, my girl. We have a lot to catch up on." She pats the bed alongside her.

I should've known. I'm a dumbass to believe anything my sister says.

Suddenly, the sound of a motor starting stirs me into action. There was no other car outside the house when I arrived. A short screeching sound. Crap, my keys! *No!*

I run outside and see the car lurch forward in a series of jerks. I stand helpless as my suitcase, cash, bank cards… fucking everything, drives off with Christina.

Fuck. I feel for my wedding dress pocket, the one design feature I insisted on. I pull out my red velvet purse. It holds the secret stash I always carry.

Guess my challenging sister has taught me one thing. *Be prepared.*

But a cell phone, essential ID, and two hundred cash aren't gonna get me far.

* * *

"Zoe, she'll be back. Things changed while you were gone. She's changed."

I drop my head in despair. What hope do I have? Mom will never see how Christina really is.

"Sure. Seems like a lot has changed from where I stand. She just stole my car and all my belongings!"

"Calm down, let me talk. You always think you know best."

"Why's Christina always your favorite, no matter what? It's unbelievable."

"Don't be silly. You know I don't have a favorite-"

A loud knock sounds. Mom doesn't move.

It sounds again, louder this time.

"Are you going to get that? I can't face anyone right now."

"Zoe. I can't."

"Can't what?"

"I can't answer the door." She flicks back the blanket covering her legs. Her right leg is in a cast reaching from her ankle to just below the knee.

"Oh my goodness! What happened?"

"Fractured fibula." She shakes her head sadly. "I didn't even fall far, just slipped on the front step and that was it. Then I needed surgery to align the bones…I have crutches but I'm not very good with those."

"That's terrible, Mom!" How does she manage? She doesn't look very fit, no doubt she would struggle to lift herself onto crutches.

Bashing on the door now. *Fine.*

I wrench the door open to find a couple of kids. Well, one of the girls looks like a teenager. She's with a little girl, barely four years old.

"We don't want to buy anything, thanks." I start to swing the door back.

"Ha, cool joke," the teen says flatly. "It's just fifty for today. Hey, I don't think I've ever seen you in a dress before."

She hands me a child's pink backpack. I take it, not sure what to say. She sticks out her palm expectantly, as the little girl pushes past me and runs inside.

It's then I notice the bright auburn streak in the child's hair. Weird, that's how mine and Christina's hair was before turning vibrant red.

I fumble in my pocket, take out my purse, and hand the girl a fist full of tens.

"Cool, thanks, Christina." She pockets the cash. "Bye, Summer!"

My head is reeling. My instinct is telling me this tiny child is Christina's.

She has a child? And she just left her? I walk back to Mom's bedroom, hardly believing what my heart is telling me.

She's gorgeous. Yes, only around three or four. Pale skin, freckles, hazel eyes, and long curly hair.

She hops on the bed and slides next to Mom, happily chatting. She looks at me and quickly buries her head into Mom's shoulder. Hmm, she certainly didn't get her shyness from her mother.

"Summer, say hello to your aunt." Mom prompts.

"Hi, Aunt Zoe, Mommy said you'll take care of me until she comes back."

Holy hell. This can't be happening.

"Hi Summer, well what a surprise to meet you!"

Mom whispers something in Summer's ear. She nods and jumps up, running past me towards the kitchen.

Now I'm really in a bind.

"Mom." I collapse onto her crocheted bed cover, "tell me Christina didn't just abandon her child!"

"Oh Zoe, don't dramatize," Mom sighs. "She'll be back. She adores that child more than life itself. I told you, she's changed. She's been sober since the day she found out she was pregnant."

"Why on earth didn't she tell me?"

"You've been gone, Zoe. You'd made it very clear you needed to be alone. Well, be without us."

Mom adjusts her glasses and looks at me intently like somehow this debacle is my doing.

"But things would've been different if I knew she had a child!"

"I guess Christina wanted a chance to see if she could do it on her own."

Well, that's one for the record books. I can't remember when Christina ever handled things independently.

"I'd like to believe that Mom. But then why did she lie to me - again? She told me you were dying! She used that story to get me here."

"I can't answer that. Maybe she thought it was the only way you'd come back."

Another thought occurs to me.

"Who's the father?"

"He's not around. And Christina refuses to say."

I want to say how typical of her that is. But I can see Mom isn't up for further conflict. There's something else on her mind.

"Zoe. Rent is due Thursday."

Ah. Here we go. Christina skipping out when responsibilities pile up is not a new thing.

"Can't you delay it, just until we get this Christina situation resolved?"

"I'm already six months behind." Mom rubs her temple and I notice the white strands through her fine hair. "The new owners have been understanding, but everyone has bills to pay, I guess. If I miss more payments, I might lose the house."

Shit! This does not sound good. "How much is due Thursday?" I wonder anxiously.

"Five hundred dollars. We've tried, Zoe. But the medical bills just keep coming, and Christina has been working day and night at the bar to make ends meet."

"You don't mean...?" Now I see what Jacob meant when he said he knows Christina. And why that drunk was so shocked I wasn't her.

"Pouring drinks and kitchen work, not selling her body;" Mom laughs.

I give a tight smile.

"We're okay for now. Why don't you get out of that wedding dress you obviously don't wanna talk about? Change into your sister's clothes. Maybe go get to know your niece."

Me? Wearing my sister's clothes? Christina is totally into showing off her curves. I'm definitely not.

"I'd sooner wear your clothes, Mom."

She smiles and reaches for the folded laundry on the edge of the bed. She throws me a knitted cardigan and floral leggings.

Hmm, careful what you wish for... I put them on anyway, it's chilly in this house. And I'm not asking about the heating when rent is overdue.

I find Summer at the dining table. She's munching on a cookie and head deep in her *Frozen* themed coloring book. Purple and green snowman…well, why not?

"Aunt Zoe? When's Mommy coming home?"

Oh, that little voice. So sweet. I feel terrible for her. "Hopefully, soon. Did Mommy tell you any secrets about when she's coming back?"

She shakes her head and sniffles.

"She only said she would be back before my next birthday."

"When is your birthday, sweetie?"

"I just had my party on Saturday. My next birthday is a long time."

She starts to cry. I have no clue what to say or do.

"But Mommy said *before*, so you won't have to wait all the way till your next birthday." I sit down next to her.

Summer climbs onto my lap and snuggles into me.

"You feel like Mommy. I like you. You won't leave me too, will you?"

Tears prick my eyes. How could I break this child's heart a second time?

"No sweetie, I'm staying right here till Mommy gets back. You'll see, she'll be back before you know it, and I bet she calls you real soon."

Well, *that's that*. Tomorrow, I'm going back to the bar to ask Jacob for my sister's job. I'll have to suck it up big time. Wear her clothes, with all the men thinking I'm Christina. Lord, give me the strength to get through this…

And then there's the giant problem of Jacob Grant.

My life in a nutshell. Sex-god of my dreams offering himself up and I have to say no because of family shit.

Every good thing I've ever had…almost had…Christina and her impeccable timing fucked up on me. Why can't I, just one time, make the decision my heart wants to make?

CHAPTER 4

JACOB

"Zoe!" I sit bolt upright in bed. Sweat-soaked sheet, heart pounding. The nightmare crowds my waking brain. I suck in several deep breaths. Fuck…just a nightmare. Not real.

It's the recurring theme, but a little different this time. Scarily different.

Bianca at the church laughing at me. Then her face morphing into Zoe. Seconds later, Zoe running up the road, crying, shots fired.

And I see him, the one bounty I never brought in. He's running after Zoe, gunning her down from behind and I can't do anything except scream her name. I'm frozen on the spot.

She falls. He turns to me and nods. "Told you I'd find you." He hisses.

Then he laughs.

That bastard still haunts me, even in death. Brock Barden was declared dead. But a body was never found. Seems I'm the only one who is worried about that fact.

Always a gruesome nightmare. Always with him in it. The addition of Zoe makes me feel ill.

I get out of bed to get some water. I need to get out of this bar, this town altogether. Fucking sitting duck. And if he thinks I'm involved with anyone, care about anyone…I'm likely signing their death warrant.

Hurry up and sell. Then disappear. Alone. No ties, no one to get involved in Barden's sick game. If he tracks me down, I'll be alone. And so be it.

Zoe leaving last night is a blessing in disguise. I can never get close to her. Never feel her lush curves press against me again. The further away she stays from me the better. And the faster I can leave Hillsdale, the better.

Sure, maybe it's a convenient way to justify my solo existence. Maybe I'm as delusional as the authorities think I am…

But was I going to take the risk? Not a fucking hope. Three years since his supposed death and since I stopped bounty hunting. Two of those years I believed he was dead.

Then, something Dad said once about a stranger in town. Mentioned he was a navy guy. Said his son was too. Didn't think much of it at the time. Apparently, the stranger never said much more, just finished his drink and left.

That rang alarm bells for me. Too much coincidence usually isn't. I just stayed away from here as much as possible. Too long, missed time with Dad.

Maybe I'm overthinking this. Just rattled because the dream included Zoe.

Perhaps the last laugh for Barden is to have me think he's out there, waiting and watching.

Still drenched from the nightmare, I splash water over my face and look at my reflection. Am I going crazy? Could any of these fears become a reality?

Steering clear of Zoe is an easy answer. She's not planning on sticking around long anyway. One less complication to deal with.

* * *

If I have to explain that sign in the window one more damn time today…and it's only midday.

Why can't anyone understand that I'm not my father? I don't owe them a living and I just want to be off-grid and left alone.

I should just shut it down, but the soft spot in me doesn't want Dad's entire staff, who he called family, left without a job. I need to keep his legacy of kindness.

Plus, boarding the place up will take longer and cause more problems. Better to sell.

I check my watch. Christina is due to start work at two o'clock. She should be here soon. Then I can take a break from all this questioning about selling up.

Christina was so good with my dad. Made him laugh a lot. He even admired her for the way she flirts with all the guys. He told me she knows exactly how to balance flirty banter with keeping guys in line.

Whatever it is, it brings in a lot of extra business. She's no dummy. She knows happy egos buy more beer and stay longer. Not to mention the extra tips.

Right on cue, I hear a couple of regulars yell her name.

Then, her presence beside me.

"Hey, Christina."

"Ah…hi."

I look up. "Zoe?"

What the heck? Last person I expected to see today. Can't

say I'm disappointed. As much as I want to feel nothing, that's not happening.

Maybe she's had a change of heart? Decided to continue what we started last night after all…

But then I notice her deep frown. She looks like she has more to worry about than me having the hots for her.

"Okay. Jacob, here's the thing. I need Christina's job.

What the hell?

"I need the money, otherwise, we can't make rent next week, and Mom will get evicted."

I watch her eyes fill with tears, her chin trembling.

My heart almost stops beating. I can't stand seeing her like this. I want to gather her in my arms and tell her everything will be okay. But no. This is trouble.

Just pat her on the back and send her on her way.

"Where's Christina? Is she sick?"

Her deep green eyes bore into me, triggering my body to throb in need. Damn.

"No. She's super healthy. So healthy, in fact, she just took off with my car, my cash, and my clothes last night." Her voice pitches a little higher, "So, unfortunately, she isn't sick."

Shit. What the fuck is Christina thinking? The last thing I need is to get into their family drama. Keep every answer at *no*.

"So long story short, I have Mom and my niece to look after, and rent to pay next week. So, Jacob. I've come to ask for Christina's job." She looks at the floor. Clearly disturbed by needing to ask me.

I just stare at her as she pitches her gaze right at me again. She kinda looks a little crazy. Her eyes shine with determination. Slightly messy red hair…I wonder if it looks like that after…

"I'm a quick learner, and I'm great with numbers, so office work is okay too." She practically dares me to say no with a look of sheer defiance in her eyes.

Against all my better judgment...and because I'm stupid, I blunder on in.

"Have you worked at a bar before?"

"No, a coffee shop. Either way, I can handle it. Also, if Christina is owed any money, I'll take that. I need three hundred and fifty dollars more to make Thursday's rent." Now anger bubbles into her words. Her small hands clench to fists at her side.

I stroke my beard, buying time. How can I put this without getting a kick in the nuts?

"Thing is, Christina is awesome at getting tips. It's just minimum wage here. Well…you know, she's your sister, so you understand how she gets those tips. I'm not sure that's your…style, though." Fuck, could things get more awkward?

Christina is a natural flirt. As my dad noted, she never steps over the line, and she definitely never accepts payment for being extra *friendly*, but she has an openly sexual way about her that men love.

Zoe is different. But I can't pay her more just so she can pay rent.

Zoe squares her shoulders and juts her chin. "Just give me the job. Let me worry about how to get tips."

"Okay, well…how about a trial-run first? See how you do."

If I've learned anything over the years, it's don't get in the way of a woman on a mission. But I also know unkept promises only end in pain. Had plenty of first-hand experience there.

"Deal." She grins, grabbing my hand to shake it.

Wow, her smile certainly lights the room.

"Start in an hour? I'll juggle some things around so I can run you through bar service. If you can handle that, you'll get through the rest."

Well, this is a bad idea. Having Zoe this close to me every day…But there's no way I could see her go without when she needs to support her family. Guess my chat with up above fell on deaf ears. Nothing surprising there.

"Look, I gotta mention. This place is on the market. I'm meeting with buyers. No guarantees, but I hope to have it sold and be out of here in four weeks." No point bullshitting. She can take it or leave it.

I watch her consider this new information. She looks just like Christina, but also so very different. Christina and I are buddies, I don't feel one speck of chemistry. But Zoe's the whole damn science experiment.

"I'll worry about four weeks, in four weeks. Right now, I need the money."

"I'll see you back here in an hour then. Look for these blue shirts in Christina's closet," I pinch my shirt, "Christina never wears them, but I gave her five anyway." Yeah, back when Dad was alive and I was pretending I'd be running this place after he was gone.

"I'll find them. Thanks again." The lines on her brow smooth out and she gives a small smile. That's better.

"No problem, sorry to hear about the family drama."

Seems like I'm not the only one. Since Dad passed, I feel a huge weight of responsibility on my shoulders. So many people here miss him, and I never know what the fuck to say to them. Dad always had words of wisdom to offer. A skill I didn't inherit.

Zoe just nods and walks out, without a clue how her well-rounded ass looks in those leggings.

Man, just walk away. Off-grid life, remember?

Life surely would be a lot easier if I just said no to Zoe. But even my hard ass couldn't do that. I just have to use some self-control around her. A *lot* of self-control.

CHAPTER 5

ZOE

Well, just as embarrassing as I imagined. But mission accomplished.

Getting a job is a start. Now I need to manage the household. Summer has preschool during the week and after-school care. And Mom thinks she can manage on the weekends if I take night shifts.

I know I should call George, and explain. Maybe tomorrow. My head's overloaded right now, and I'm so not ready for that conversation.

I need to focus on my first shift. My service skills are rusty…getting decent tips might be tough. Ugg, it's all so overwhelming.

Except for Summer…Her name is appropriate, she's a ray of joy, who lights up every day.

So, I'll do whatever it takes. And my first task is finding Christina's bar shirts.

But, as I peer into the cramped closet space, I'm quickly distracted, by my Gibson guitar case. Oh, my…I lift it out and gently open the case. There she is… glowing mahogany and rosewood.

I rub my hands together and stare at my old treasure. I lift her out carefully and begin strumming my completely out-of-tune acoustic friend. Just feels right.

My spirit soars. I suddenly feel capable of anything.

This guitar was the best friend a teen girl could ever have. I've ignored my love of music for so long. Can I even remember my songs?

My fingers close around the fretboard and I sit on the bed. The guitar tucks into my lap like it's never left. Tuning her up, I recall the way singing expressed all my pain and hurt. It made me brave and daring. Like I could have it all.

But…that's a dangerous feeling. Because it leads to stupid decisions and terrible disappointment. Like almost signing a music contract.

I fell for all the music producer's hype. His smooth words were a trap, and I stupidly fell in.

Not my finest moment. He wasn't even planning on signing me up. For a month of our joke romance, he claimed I was his '...one and only, never met anyone like you…,' true love.

Yeah right…then I overheard him one day, saying sex with me was 'boring as hell,' and that he was going to seek out some '...real rock chicks.' I discovered he wasn't a producer at all. It was all a bullshit scam.

How foolish I felt. Thinking he loved me.

Back then, I packed my guitar away and swore I'd never let someone gain control like that again.

Christina was struggling then too. In a downward spiral of self-destruction. I couldn't turn to her for support. I decided I was done with this town and left.

I moved to Ann Arbor, studied at business school, and worked evenings at a coffee shop.

And that's where I met George. A solid, reliable guy. And a banker. Actually, he was managing a major bank at just thirty years old.

He had it all figured out. And a sharp, logical mind. I found his methodical way of thinking very attractive. He gave me stability, comfort, and routine.

Ok. There was no spark. I never felt a deep love for him. No fireworks. But it was nice, pleasant. A warm feeling I could build on. I could love him in time. Or so I hoped.

Whenever I doubted my decision, there was my irresponsible twin to reinforce it for me. I never wanted her crazy life, always struggling to get by. I wanted to prove to Christina there was a better way to go about life.

Now, I'm not so sure she isn't right. Living life on the edge. Not giving a damn. Somehow, she always lands back on her feet.

But me, always careful to make the right choices…well, I just keep getting kicked in the guts.

Hm. Maybe it's time to take a risk. Hell, a few of Dolly and Tammy's classics, that might get the tips flowing.

That's it! After my shift tonight, I'll test out the acoustics in the bar. When everyone's gone. I'll probably forget every word, but I have to try. With Mom's fridge woefully devoid of fresh food, and a little girl to care for, there's no time to lose.

If it's good enough, I'll ask Jacob. Maybe he'll let me play a few nights a week.

Wow, just thinking about him makes me shiver. *Get it together, Zoe*. I have to learn to ignore those feelings.

Anyway, there's no time to be mooning over a man who is

selling out the very soul of Hillsdale. But that's Jacob's worry, not mine. He can duke it out with the locals.

* * *

My first bar service and I spend most of it reminding the locals that Christina has a twin.

And they soon discover I'm not into flirting and talking smack like my sister.

Which is fine…Except they all leave right after Monday night football and my tips aren't exactly life-changing.

I guess forty pity dollars is better than nothing. And it was hard-earned since I spent most of the night trying not to get too close to Jacob. It messed with my head that we kept gravitating to the same place, as if in sync.

At least he's professional. In fact, he's almost too polite and nice. Meanwhile, I really just want to drag him out the back into that storage room.

But I can push those feelings aside. It's just physical after all, nothing more.

Thankfully, when I offered to finish the cleaning checklist, he eventually agreed and headed upstairs. Now, I just need to lock up and keep the keys for my morning shift tomorrow.

A day shift will give me a chance to chat with Willy. He runs the kitchen and can answer all my questions about the menu. I recall getting better tips back at the coffee shop in Ann Arbor just by recommending one of the specialty dishes.

Now the bar is dark and quiet. I grab my guitar from inside the back entrance, where I stowed it earlier. I'm a little excited because the acoustics here will be amazing. But I have to keep it quiet. Last thing I need is Jacob overhearing.

I pull up a chair in the far corner, strum the strings, and

adjust the tuning. I can't even think of what to sing. I attempt a couple of lines of *Jolene*. Eww. So rusty. They'll be paying me to stop at this rate.

I remember the song the fake producer wanted to fake-sign me up with. It's a love song. A full-on tear-jerker, torn heartstrings, desperado, love song. *Can I do it?*

I quietly strum the first chord and the second, then the third. The rhythm comes back to me right away. The lyrics emerge…I stumble over a couple, then breathe in deeply. Come on girl, you've got rent to pay, and need to put food on the table.

Finally, the words begin to flow. And it feels great. My heart fills with gratitude.

How could I think giving up singing was the right choice? *I need this*. The emotions flow through the song and through me, like a powerful healing force.

The first chorus hits me hard. Tears well, and I choke a little. I grab that raw emotion and try to channel it into the lyrics.

That works. I close my eyes and the creative force runs through me, through my guitar. And when I open my eyes, he's there.

Jacob. Looking at me with a dark intensity that penetrates me to the core.

I should stop.

But I don't.

Standing there in his blue jeans, bare-chested. And man, that chest is compelling. His tight abs lead down to a perfectly etched triangle, before the top of his low-slung denims interrupt the view. There's an eagle tattoo across his chest. Another tatt lower down…

Focus on the song, not his insane body.

I go into the second verse. A little louder this time, letting my voice do its thing. Jacob steps closer.

I hold eye contact and finish the verse, then launch into the chorus again. My eyes close as I hit the top note, and I let my voice fall back down to the lower note.

His hand brushes my cheek. I don't dare open my eyes.

I want him *so bad*, I can't trust myself to look at him.

He takes the guitar and pulls me up from my seat. I open my eyes. I wish I hadn't.

Deep desire burns in his dark eyes. He's touching my face again, his thumb tracing my bottom lip. He bends lower and kisses my neck. His lips are so hot, they burn a track in my skin.

He pulls me against him. He's rock-hard and I don't resist.

Because I want this. I want him to make me forget everything.

I trace my hands over his powerful shoulders and through his beard. It's less scratchy than I imagined. His lips feel soft against my fingertips, and I pull him into the explosive kiss I've been craving.

He doesn't disappoint. His mouth takes over mine in a swirl of heat and need.

"Zoe," he breathes, "I want you. *Now*." The rough edge of his voice melts me. "Please don't stop me this time." He scoops me up in his arms. Kissing me still.

My arms instinctively wrap around his neck, and I nuzzle into his muscled shoulders. His masculine pheromones intoxicate me. I can't stop. I've lost control. And I don't care.

He takes the stairs two at a time, carrying me, groaning my name. He kicks the door open and stumbles to the bed. Blood surges in my veins, my pulse is thumping in my ears.

I take him in my arms and deepen the kiss, melding my body tightly to his. I've never known lust like this.

I let my hands explore every part of him I can reach. Just this once, I really want to let myself go and follow my heart.

I know there's no future in giving my body to him. But damn, I just want to feel what real passion is like, once in my life.

I push upwards, and he leans back. If I am doing this once, I'll give it everything I have. I slowly unbutton my shirt and let it slide down my shoulders and onto the floor.

Good idea, choosing one of Christina's bras. Even the tamest pieces in her lingerie drawer are ten times sexier than any of mine. From the look on Jacob's face, this may be the only time in my adult life I have something to thank her for.

He sucks in a long breath as he watches me undress. His hunger is evident as he clenches his fists like he's trying to keep his hands off me. "Keep going." His rugged voice commands.

I wiggle my hips and push the jeans below my hips, down my thighs…and then he's on me, helping to release me completely. Little more than a growl sounds from him as his huge hands span each of my hips and he pulls me close.

I throb in places I'd never known could throb. Heaven help me, how I want this man.

"Zoe. You're so beautiful. Let me show you…" He flips me to the mattress, on my back. He fumbles in a drawer, mutters about being safe, and is back beside me in a flash.

His jeans are straining. I sit up, and reach to unzip him. This appears too much for him. As he breaks free from the restraint, I gasp at the sight before me.

I lie back as Jacob all but rips my panties from my body. I blush deeply as he pushes my thighs open and stares at me like a hungry wolf. Oh my…never before…

There is absolutely nothing that can stop the momentum of this train. Electricity surges through my body, as he lowers his mouth between my thighs.

All I can hear is my voice screaming his name, as my world implodes. I'm done for. I'll never be the same again.

CHAPTER 6

JACOB

I wake up and Zoe's not here. What time is it? Six. Damn, she left early. And I slept through. *Nice one, Jacob.*

But maybe it's for the best. Clearly, she isn't into affection and pillow talk. She's not trying to make this into a relationship. Great. Too easy.

Definitely better this way. Now I just have to find a way to act normal around her when she's working.

Well, it's no big deal. Just sex. Just mind-blowing, atomic sex. That's all. I'm not making a big deal out of it.

Wait a minute…I slept through? I slept through! No nightmares. At least none that woke me up in a panicked sweat. That's the first time in…shit. I try to recall the last time I'd slept soundly till morning.

All my nights with Bianca, no matter how exhausted from lovemaking…I still woke up agitated and haunted by my bad dreams.

Just a coincidence. Because Zoe and I…well, just coincidence.

Last night was something else. With Zoe everything felt explosive. Like I couldn't get enough of her taste, her smell… her eagerness. Our bodies fit perfectly. I can't explain it.

Luckily, I don't have to. She's not here, so that means it's nothing special for her, right?

And that's fine by me, my mind needs to focus on the big picture. I flick the shower pressure up high. Time to clean up my act, and get prepared. This may be the day I finally sell this place.

Zoe will open the bar at ten. I've scheduled a couple of experienced staff too. They'll show her the ropes. And I don't have to try and keep my hands off her. Win-win.

Instead, I'm going to meet a very serious buyer. A banker left a message yesterday afternoon. Said he may be interested in buying the place. Only problem is he needs someone to run it. That's really not an option for me.

But maybe I can find someone. Whatever it takes. I'm so ready to get this place sold and get back to a simple life. Being with Zoe was amazing, but it's just complicating the fuck out of everything now. I need to get my head on straight again.

Every muscle in my body is sore. We didn't hold anything back last night.

Something about Zoe makes me want her so bad. Her singing last night sent my desire sky high. I couldn't resist touching her. That sultry voice, those gorgeous green eyes… full, sweet lips. And that long flaming, red hair against her pale skin.

Shit, I'm working myself into a lather just thinking about her.

Once I kissed her, there was no turning back. Even though there's every reason why I shouldn't have touched her.

It's strange…Christina looks exactly the same, wears half

the clothing, and flirts like hell, yet I've never even had an inkling of desire for her. And I still can't believe she left her kid. Summer is all she ever talks about.

That's family for ya. Can't live with 'em, can't shoot 'em.

Anyway, it's a two-hour drive to Ann Arbor. I need to get my books in order because that banker is gonna want those numbers nailed down tight.

* * *

"Mr. Grant. Sorry to keep you waiting. I'm George Miller."

I shake his hand. "No problem, George. Call me Jacob."

"Come into my office, Jacob. Coffee, tea?"

"Coffee sounds great. Cream no sugar." I could drink a gallon of the stuff right now. I pull at my collar. Button-up things annoy the shit out of me.

"Felicity, can you get us coffee?" George shoots the order to his assistant.

"Yes, of course."

I turn to her and give a nod of thanks. I'm rewarded with an over the glasses bedroom eyes look. Must be the sports jacket. If I hadn't just had the best sex ever with Zoe, I'd maybe give her a sniff of hope.

But not today. Today is about selling the bar. Then, I'll find a property far away from Hillsdale. Where no one knows my name.

George's office blows me away. It's huge. Floor to ceiling windows overlook the whole goddamned city. I walk over and take in the view. Cannot understand how people can live on top of each other. Not my thing, that's for sure.

I'm not sure *banker* is an accurate term for George Miller. Nothing here looks fake or cheap. He seems like he is way up in the chain…literally. Strange he referred to himself as a banker on the phone.

I guess I should be happy. Looks like there'll be no problem raising cash to buy the bar.

"Take a seat, Jacob. Spectacular view, isn't it?"

I sit in the soft leather chair opposite him. "Sure is. I'm guessing you're a little more than a banker?"

George gives a tight smile. "You could say that. I've been in finance a long time."

"How did you hear about the bar being for sale?"

"I was driving through the town a couple nights ago and saw the sign in the window. Tell me why you're selling?"

Felicity enters with the coffee tray. Setting it on the desk she gives me a warm smile before leaving. But most of my attention is on George, and what his agenda might be.

I contemplate how much to tell him. "The bar belonged to my dad. He passed away recently. I'm looking for a quieter existence."

"Quieter than Hillsdale? Does that even exist?" He grins as he pours his coffee. "Here, help yourself."

"Thanks." I take the coffee and smile back at him, like I've got nothing to hide. "I'm after fewer people and more wilderness."

"I see." He adjusts some papers on his desk. "Forgive me. I like to do proper due diligence with any major purchases. Not looking to buy trouble."

He eyes me intently. "So, you're not interested in sticking around? If I buy the bar?"

"Don't get me wrong, George. I love the place… but it was my dad's thing. He had a way with people." I wonder why he cares so much about what my plan is after the sale. Is this common with the bank's due diligence?

Seems weird. I sip my coffee. It tastes expensively smooth and bold. So good.

"I understand. I got into banking because of my father too. While this business has been very good to me, sometimes I wish I could've just said I'm going fishing or something."

Ah, so he's just imagining how life would be if he'd followed his heart, not his head. I can tell you that for free...*Hurtsville.*

"Anyway. I digress. You're looking to sell the bar for a little over three hundred thousand. Seems a little high for such a small town."

George sips his coffee and leans back into his oversized chair. It's a weird egg shape, with a large, curved headrest. Guess it's some kind of expensive European design. Makes him look a lot like that *Dr. Evil* movie character.

His eyes stay fixated on me.

Here we go. I guess he wants me to give the place away for nothing, so he can knock it down and build something else. I hand him my folder.

"Got the numbers here to back up the asking price. The bar is in a central location and gets all the local trade, including roughnecks from the outlying ranches and oil fields. Plus, plenty of travelers passing through. They want good food and cold beer. Which is exactly what they find, and why they keep coming back."

George raises his eyebrows as he scans the first page of my documents. "Very impressive figures. I'm not sure I'd be so quick to part with a business making such a good profit."

"You aren't parting with it, I am. I have other reasons." I'm a bit irritated by his personal line of questioning. I'm not on trial, I'm selling a bar.

"Indeed. Money isn't everything, so I've heard." George continues to page through my documents. "What about your employees? What if I close it down? Do you care what happens to them?"

For the love of – "With all due respect George, I don't see how that's of any concern to you. Either you're interested or you're not. Let me worry about the rest."

Just because he's rich doesn't mean he gets to know what I care about. I feel like saying, *just buy it or fuck off.* I'm in no mood for time-wasters.

He has a chuckle. "You're quite right. Let's just cut to the chase. I'm looking to broaden my investment portfolio. This looks like a good investment.

"However, I really want you to stay on for at least six months until we can find a suitable replacement to manage it."

"It's just not an option for me, sorry."

"Of course, I would provide an attractive retention package for you to stay on. It would only put your plans off for another six months, and you'll have more cash to play with."

"I really don't think you understand."

"Don't decide right now. Take my offer under consideration. Do what you can to build up the bar and clientele. Employ more staff. Whatever it takes."

He hands me a large yellow envelope. "Open this later. For now, think about the possibility of staying on. At least for the short term. I'm only asking for six months of your time and a solid offer of purchase to follow."

I take the envelope. This guy looks like he's used to getting his way. And I've come up against his type before. All placid business in the front, but gangster in the back. More strategic to go along with it right now.

I still have contacts in National Intelligence. I'll check

him out in my own way. Because when my neck hairs bristle like this, something's always up.

It's one thing to want to sell the bar, but another thing is to sell out to illegal activities. My gut churns.

"Thanks, George. Don't mind me, I've been a little edgy since my dad passed. I'll give your offer good consideration, and get back to you by next week."

"Perfect." George stands up and offers his hand.

I accept the handshake. *Play the game*. "Great. Nice to meet you."

"And you, Jacob."

He hits the intercom, and I turn to see Felicity in the doorway, eyeballing me again.

"Felicity will show you out, Jacob."

And I'll be checking you out, George Miller. I'm not sure what you're hiding, but I know I'm not getting the full story. *Yet*.

CHAPTER 7

ZOE

I'm stuck in this crazy limboland. All of my belongings are either lost with Christina, or back in the city. Wearing my own clothes would at least help me feel more grounded.

A raid of Christina's laundry hamper turned up the work shirts and more jeans- even a couple of pairs that aren't full of trashy rips. But I really don't want to wear her clothes. Not only are they not my style, but they also remind me of our contentious clothing wars.

Even Mom's interventions to color code, or otherwise separate our stuff didn't solve the issue. Poor Mom. We really gave her a workout.

Summer brings back many of my childhood memories of Christina. Somehow, what should have been happy moments, always got lost in bickering. Sounds trivial now that I think about it. It was like she was jealous of me.

Anyway, clothes should be the least of my worries.

Because there's the George situation…There's Mom's

care to organize every day. And I'm praying Christina will call. For Summer's sake at least.

So many things make my brain hurt.

One thing at a time.

I opened the bar this morning with the help of Maddie, the other bartender, and Harriet, the cleaner. They're both lovely, even if a little exhausting with their constant amazement at how identical Christina and I look. *Tell me something new.*

They've even called me Christina a couple of times. But that's to be expected. At least they will never have to deal with my sister and me in the same room. I kind of wish I never did either. But then again, I need her back to relieve me of some of these responsibilities.

Shit, Christina, and responsibilities…two things that are usually completely at odds.

I check the time. Ten minutes of my break left. Next up, is cocktail training with Maddie. Since lunch service's done, we have a few hours to practice while the bar's quiet.

As much as I didn't want to see Jacob after last night, this place feels so empty without him.

I'd snuck out of his bed around five, to be home when Summer woke up. Her mother left her…the least her aunt can do is give her some sense of security.

Jacob was out cold when I left. Which was for the best. I couldn't be sure I could say *no* to his ever-hard body and demanding kisses.

Sex last night was a definite one-off. Just something we both needed. Not happening again. Because I'm committed to taking care of the family until Christina gets back.

All I need from Jacob now is this job, and a chance to perform my songs. I definitely need to reel in extra tips. And singing may be my best chance.

My shift ends at five, just as happy hour kicks off. I hope

then Jacob will let me play a few songs…at least to try it out. But I have no intention of my music serving as foreplay this time.

God, how can I face him again? I'm scared I'll blush like crazy and everyone within a ten-foot radius will know our secret.

I still ache in places I never knew existed. And I crave him. Crave to get lost in the way he touches me. To feel that electricity, as he works his way all over my body with his mouth.

He took me beyond anywhere I'd ever been. His sheer size, and his obvious desire, carried me to the heights of ecstasy.

But I know there's no future in it.

Sure, the sex was amazing. But Jacob isn't looking for commitment, and neither am I. Ha, with my mess of a life? Who on earth would want that baggage? And I certainly don't have room for another person's needs.

And it's not like we even really know each other. A few sketchy details, and that's it.

That's why I'm not even asking where he is today. Though I can't help picking up on the gossip around here. And boy, there are a ton of rumors and bad blood about the bar being sold.

Most people are shocked. They honestly thought Jacob was here to stay. A few seem to understand he has his own life to live. Employees are rightfully worried about their jobs. And other locals are scared about what selling this place means for the town.

Because if this bar closes, Hillsdale could practically become a ghost town. And what if it's demolished for a new development? Well, that would just about break everyone's heart. Poor Jacob. It'll be no small task navigating the emotions of his local clientele. Maybe that's a good reason to perform a few country classics tonight. Music might help soothe the collective nerves a bit.

And that's all good. As long as I can make some money.

Really, life can be such a bitch. I'd almost forgotten the stress of living day to day, paycheck to paycheck. Money was never an issue when I was with George. With a property portfolio like his, financial worries are null and void.

Not that I didn't pay my way. I worked hard and took care of all my personal needs. I hate feeling like I owe anyone anything.

But still, George created a security bubble around me, so I almost forgot what it was like to struggle. All my family concerns went into hibernation. I liked that downtime from the trauma and troubles of my sister.

Sadly, the way George organized everything, so I barely had to think for myself, is the reason I couldn't marry him. Life was just so…routine.

Everything had turned to beige, and I needed some color back. Maybe that's why last night felt so intense…all those months without any intimacy with my fiancé…

But that's no excuse for what I did. I would never have jilted him except Christina's fake crisis provided the opportunity.

Shit, it was only three days ago. It feels like a lifetime now.

I'm not sure he'll ever forgive me. But that doesn't mean I shouldn't own my mistake and apologize to him anyway.

I'll call him. Tomorrow. Not anything I can handle right now.

* * *

Fidgety as fuck. What's going on with me? All of a sudden, I have clammy palms and a dry mouth. I just gotta hope this performance goes well.

Jacob is back. The butterflies in my stomach start to stir as I watched him go upstairs. He's wearing a white collared shirt and a jacket over his arm. I'm not used to the corporate look on him, but he sure wears it well.

I get tingles thinking about how he looks without all those layers.

Seeing him after last night is going to be both exhilarating and awkward. I know we're adults, but I like to keep my private life private. The other staff definitely can't know what went on between us. And he'll likely be back for the evening rush, especially with the small crowd already milling around the bar.

"Hey, Zoe…"

"Ya, Maddie?"

Maddie's a little younger than me. Maybe twenty-two. She's pretty hip for a small-town girl. Tattoos, eyebrow and nose piercings, bright blue streak in her hair. She's a skilled bartender and everybody warms to her vibrant energy.

"Is Christina coming back soon?"

My neck tenses. "Um…hard to say. Hope so." Did I need to have this conversation? Hell no. But then again, maybe I can get some inside info.

Maddie continues topping up the cocktail garnishes. "I know she spoke about going to nursing school, but I thought that was happening next week."

I can't help it, an incredulous laugh bursts out of me. *Nursing school*? Christina? Maddie must have her mixed up with someone else. God, as if she would commit to studying anything, let alone a caring vocation like that.

"Look, I really don't have any answers on my sister's thought process."

"You don't get along?"

"You could say that." That and a hundred other things, all of them expletives.

"Funny, she said she wants to get into nursing to be more like you."

More like me! What a crock of shit.

"Yeah, sure she did."

Christina who spent almost all our adult lives screaming about how she'd never, ever want to be as uptight as me.

"She talks a lot about how you are the straight one-eighty and she's…Well, she's Christina," Maddie laughs.

"Can't argue with that."

"Anyway, I hope she's back soon. I miss her. Her energy is contagious, ya know?"

"Something like that." I've never caught anything but her bad energy, that's for sure.

"I get it. Christina gets judged negatively sometimes. And, I can relate. I often wonder what it would be like without my tatts and piercings. Not to have attention on me every time I go out. But I guess I'll never know, and that's okay."

"You could wear long sleeves, a hat, and take your piercings out for a day."

"Um, that's a hard *no*. You sound like my parents," Maddie laughs again. Her laugh is contagious.

I grin at her. She's very likable. "Christina and I are opposites in every way. But I hope we become friends one day."

"She's great at being a friend. The best."

This I didn't expect. Christina never had close friends. She was too busy being consumed by thoughts about herself to care about anyone else. But I guess she had to be friendly with people she saw every day at work.

"Not interrupting any work, am I?" His deep tone takes me by surprise...oh and there go the butterflies again. I don't dare turn around and look at him.

"Ha! Never. I've mastered the *look like you're working but actually not* mode now, Boss," Maddie grins at Jacob over my shoulder.

I can feel him behind me. I try to calm my nerves which are running wild. Shit. Can't I ever be cool about anything?

"Hi, Jacob." Now I sound like a robot. Still not turning around, I try to focus on drying the glass in my hand.

"Hell, Maddie. You could learn a thing or two about productivity from Zoe…I know I have."

I spin around just as he winks and walks away.

Holy freak! Did he just say that? I'm gonna die right here on the spot. My face burns hotter than the sun. Way to go, ice queen, your cool facade lasted five seconds.

But why would he say that in front of Maddie? I know we went hard at it last night, more than once, but surely he doesn't promote his sex life to his staff…?

Maddie throws me a crooked grin. "Oh, I get it. Christina wants to be more straight like you, and you're here getting a little dirty action. Good work!"

I must look completely horrified. I'm speechless.

"It's okay. He's already left. I'm sure he just meant the way you work around here." She's still laughing. "I wouldn't worry, everyone has two sides. You and Christina just choose to show one of them, doesn't mean you don't have the other. No shame in either one."

How can I even answer that little philosophical bombshell?

She steps forward and grabs my humiliated face in her

warm hands. "Zoe…Speak! It's fine. You're human." She laughs again and I can't help it. I start laughing too.

"Wow. Sorry."

"Nothing to be sorry for. He busted outta here like he had a dog on his ass. He realized what he said too." More laughing. "Made for each other you two are. Subtle as a herd of elephants."

"Well, I think I'll just focus on the job at this point."

"I'm off anyway. My shift is done, and I can't spend all night torturing you two, though I'd like to."

"Wait, you're leaving? What about closing?"

"Jacob said he was on the late shift. In more ways than one, I guess."

"Oh stop it. I *can't even* with you right now." I roll my eyes.

Maddie backs away with her hands held high in surrender. "I'm out, all good. Don't hurt me." Then she points behind me and silently mouths, "*He's behind you*."

CHAPTER 8

JACOB

Fuck, the look on Zoe's face when I blurted out about her work *productivity*. Even after I said it, I could hear my tone could easily be taken out of context. I could've toasted a marshmallow off that red face. In my defense, I didn't mean it *that* way.

She looked so embarrassed…

Maybe she doesn't want to have sex with me again. Maybe I disappointed her?

Ha! As if. Those screams weren't from disappointment. Her body clinging to mine wasn't a display of disappointment. Never disappointed a woman in bed. Never actually occurred to me I might either. Till now. Shit. Stop lurking around and say something to her.

"Zoe. I didn't mean…"

"It's fine."

"I meant you're a great worker behind the bar. Not… um…anywhere else. No, you work great other ways too…so great." Fuck! Just shut up. Why can't I just ever say what I mean around her? Stupid shit just keeps coming out.

"Can we drop it? Please." Zoe gives me a touch on the arm and I get a full-body rush. I really need to check myself. So not cool.

"Thought you'd never ask." I give her a smile and her shoulders relax a little.

"It's been a good night. Quite a few people around." She's making small talk, and all I want to do is kiss that mouth.

Get a fucking grip, Jacob. "Yeah, we have changeover shifts for a few of the ranches around here mid-week, and those that travel in and out of the oil fields."

"Do you think they'd like to hear some country songs?" She's been drying the same spot on that glass forever.

"You do country stuff?" It actually isn't a bad idea. The jukebox gets a good workout on country music.

"Figure it's worth a try."

If her singing last night is anything to go by, she'll attract more than tips. I clench my fist at the thought of the men here going anywhere near her… What if she likes the look of another guy? I'll tear his head off.

Whoa. Calm down. It was just one night. You don't want a commitment, remember? Let it go.

"Is it worth a try…tonight?"

"What do you have in mind?"

Her confidence level looks low. No reason to be. But I don't want her singing that same song she sang last night. Every man will be creaming his jeans, and their women will get pissed off…and I probably will too.

"Covers of the popular jukebox songs. Nothing original." Back to polishing the same spot on the same glass.

I take the glass off her and set it on the counter. "You'll

wear a hole in that soon. Country songs are a great idea. Give it a try."

Think she'll be surprised at how quickly her tip jar fills up.

"What, right now?" She looks back at me with wide eyes.

"You can wait till everyone goes home if you like. But less tips and…we both know how that ends." Might be treading on thin ice with that wisecrack. But we can't be super serious all the time. We all need a little fun.

Zoe smiles. "Yeah…I'd much rather have the tips to be honest." Her voice sounds flat. But then she laughs.

"Sure you would. Get moving. I predict the beer will flow an extra hour while you sing."

Her wide smile lights up the room, and my insides.

Trouble is, how do I ever say no to those green eyes? I sure as hell can't say no to the natural, sultry sway of those lush hips she doesn't even know she has.

"Can you handle the bar alone?"

"What do you think? Anyway, Willie can stay back to help."

"I'll go grab my guitar from the back."

"Strum a few bars, then I'll introduce you. Because there may be a few heart attacks if our regulars think Christina is about to sing. She's not known for her vocal abilities. We nicknamed her the *Karaoke Killer*."

Zoe smiles and nods. "Sure. Yeah, by the same token, don't ever let me near a dance floor. My sister inherited all the body coordination."

Hmm, not sure about that after last night. But I manage to keep my thoughts to myself.

I bag up excess cash from the till. A lot rolled through today, and you can't be too careful. As I drop the money in the safe, I notice George's yellow envelope. He mentioned ways to develop the business. Live music could be a viable option.

But I haven't even looked at his offer yet. Don't know why. Just can't seem to open that envelope.

I serve a fresh round of drinks and go grab empty glasses from the tables. Most folks usually leave around this time, so let's see. Can't hurt to try out some live country music. No point having a stage in the corner if no one ever uses it.

Back to the bar with a full tray, just as Zoe strums her introductory chords. I tap on a glass, until the bar buzz mellows to low murmurs.

"Listen up folks. This little lady is looking to entertain you for a couple hours. If you stick around, there'll be some bar snacks on the house. I'll leave her tip jar up here." I set the jar down on the end of the bar. "Round of applause for Zoe."

There's some polite clapping.

Zoe launches straight into one of our most played jukebox songs, *Crazy*, by Patsy Cline. I guess this will make or break her.

The room falls silent, and I may be biased, but if that isn't the best thing I'd ever heard in my life…I look around the bar, full of roughnecks tonight…hard-working men and women. For a few seconds, I think it's about to empty out. Shit. I've never heard it so silent.

But then, as if the whole room let out a collective sigh of relief, smiles break out, chatter resumes, some sing along a little, and there's a surge for more drinks.

I get busy filling orders. Gradually, I notice how many people are throwing their change, and quite a bit more into Zoe's jar.

I look over and her eyes meet mine. A warm feeling rushes through me. I flick my eyes at her pile of tips and wink at her. She smiles back, and doesn't miss a beat as she transitions into the next song.

Empty glasses appear everywhere. Shit. Better crank it up a couple of gears.

A half a dozen country classics later, Willie has served up plenty of bowls of fries and onion rings, and joins me behind the bar to help pour drinks. Just as I think Zoe might need a break, a few couples hit the dance floor to her Alan Jackson cover.

Each chance I get, I watch her. Her voice is clear and strong, with an endearing vulnerability that just about breaks your heart.

Dad loved country music. And I think of him as her voice rings out, breathing life into this place. For the first time, I feel his connection to this bar.

It's not just people buying drinks. Their chatter, their laughter, their connection…It elevates people out of the mundane, and gives them a sense of belonging. This place, this bar, *Buddy's Bar* needs people. Dad left a legacy and I'd do what I could…

But I can't change who I am. This life is not for me. I don't need people. I need solitude. People make me edgy.

George wanting me to stay six more months here? Not happening. Sooner I get out, the better. No time for attachments, or friends. Or even Zoe Olsen.

I call last drinks at eleven, to the groans of everyone in the room. Zoe has sung three sets and her tip jar is overflowing with bills.

"Hey everyone. Tell your friends, Saturday night's a tribute to Buddy. Zoe will be singing Dad's favorites, and we'll all say goodbye to the old coot in style…Now get your asses home safe. I'm beat. And thanks."

As they file past the bar, plenty of patrons stop to shake

my hand. I see Zoe collecting glasses, saying thanks and goodbye to the stragglers. We finally get them all out the door, and I lock it shut.

"Sorry about the Saturday night announcement. Probably should've asked first."

But she's glowing with happiness. Radiant. I guess it must be rewarding to be able to entertain people like that.

"You may need a police escort home with all this." I point to her tip jar crammed full.

She grins so wide, I think her face will break. I recognize the relief in those tear-filled eyes.

"Right? Unbelievable. I think I can make rent just on what's in that jar right now… Jacob…" her husky voice saying my name sends my blood rushing again.

She's looking at me with those wet, glistening eyes. "Jacob, really, I can't thank you enough…"

"Oh, I think you can…" Fuck I can't help it. I reach for her and now her eyes gleam with desire. I'm no schoolboy. My mouth crushes against hers, and my need zaps through me. I'm no saint either. She's all mine tonight.

"You're something special, Zoe Olsen."

Her kiss drives me insane. Her arms circle my neck, and her lush thigh encases my hip. I deepen the kiss as I rub my hardness against her. She moans. I want her so bad, but I need to be sure we're on the same page. We break the kiss together.

"Zoe, this can't be a relationship. But fuck, *I want you*. It's up to you. If you want me to stop, just say so. This is separate from work. There will be no issues if you say no."

There, I said it.

"Last thing I want is anything serious." Her soft voice swells my loins as she brushes against my inner thigh. I feel the burn through my jeans. Who the fuck invented zippers? Man's gonna injure himself soon.

"Just sex. Consenting adults…" I barely scrape out the word as her lips and teeth graze across my neck, and down to my chest.

"No strings." She mutters against my skin. "Shut up, I want you. Now."

I manage to flick the main lights off…no passer-by is gonna see this show. We continue our rampage of each other's bodies, gradually stripping away every item of clothing. I fumble a condom from my wallet.

I take her long and slow from behind, and let her cry out as I fill her, balls-deep.

She turns around and wraps her legs around my bare hips, and her ass props on the edge of the counter. She cries out my name, and fireworks take over my brain. She knows exactly what she needs and takes it. Breaking me down in the process.

"Jacob. Don't stop."

"You're amazing." I growl into her ear, and her fingernails dig into my back. Now her legs lock hard around me, and as soon as the first shudder hits her, my control is lost.

Every ounce of oxygen is gone from my lungs by the time we let each other go.

"Shit. We need to clean this bar, and get the money into the safe." Zoe sounds as out of breath as I feel.

"Um. Yeah. That escalated quickly."

Her hand touches mine. "My fault as much as yours."

She's right though. I have to keep things in order. My feet firmly planted on the ground. But being firmly planted inside Zoe, is all I can think about when she's around.

"Jacob, truth be told, I'm just out of an engagement."

She's already spraying sanitizer across the bar top and furiously wiping away at drink stains.

Well, *that* hits a nerve. But easier to keep things simple.

"Well, serious relationships aren't for me." Not exactly true, but this is just a friends with benefits scenario. Why complicate shit?

"You've never had a serious relationship?" Her tone sounds suspect.

"None that I want to count, put it that way." I stack another tray of clean glasses away and reload the washer.

"Jacob, if we do this…whatever this is…I have to make sure I'm back home by early morning before my niece wakes up."

"Sure." She's even setting the conditions of a no-strings arrangement? Could this get any more perfect? I think fucking not.

"And you can never come to my place." Wrong! Just got more perfect.

"And we never go out in public. We know some people will suspect, but we never tell anyone. Deal?" She holds out her hand.

"Deal." I take her hand and pull her in close for another heated kiss. How can I even be close to another hard-on after what we've just done? Night for miracles it seems. Her kisses take me off this planet.

"Jacob?"

"Mmm?" I nuzzle into her neck.

"We need to finish cleaning up."

"Then go to bed?"

"Okay. Then we'll go to bed."

CHAPTER 9

ZOE

Well, it's rent day. And I have every penny of the five hundred needed! Plus, I've filled the refrigerator with healthy food.

And finally, after five days, I'm going to thoroughly search Christina's stuff to see if I can piece together a few outfits beyond jeans and t-shirts.

I still haven't spoken with George. And the thought of getting a lift back into the city to pick up some items makes me nervous.

At least Summer helps distract me from bad thoughts. She fills me with a feeling of happiness I've never felt before. It doesn't matter what I think of Christina. Summer is my niece, and I will do anything to protect her.

And today, Summer's morning cuddle was delivered with some important news. Turns out, Christina is calling her nearly every day.

Not sure why Mom didn't break this helpful information, but at least she confirmed it.

"So, is she coming back soon?" I asked her bluntly.

"She didn't really say…I guess she'll talk to you about it next time she calls. How did your performance go last night?" Mom really is adept at deflection.

The truth is, well, I'm not exactly unhappy. After less than a week here, I feel like I've been spun into an alternate reality. So much about my life, and me, is different.

For one thing, I've never had a sex life like what I'm experiencing now. And that's after just three nights in his bed…and the after-hours bar…oh, and the storage room that one time.

Now we're busy planning Buddy's tribute night. And staying away from any other future plans.

I guess I'll just try to stay working there, and performing until Christina gets back.

I know this isn't for the rest of my life. I'm learning to just take it day by day. At least the rent burden has been momentarily lifted.

As I attempt to evaluate the contents of Christina's closet for the second time, I notice Summer's beloved toy rabbit on the bed. My heart melts. Of course, Summer misses her mother terribly. But somehow, she accepts why Christina is gone. She's doing a much better job with that than me.

Recalling my conversations with Maddie and others, I can tell people genuinely miss Christina. Despite her over the top ways, no one has a bad word to say about her.

But they never had to live with her and fix her fuck-ups.

Maybe Maddie was right. Everyone has two sides, but may choose to show one side and hide another. Is that what Christina and I do?

The thought stays in the back of my mind. I'm not even sure being with Jacob *is* my bad side…it feels damn good to me and we're not hurting anyone.

Maybe not calling George is my bad side. Ah, I don't know, I'm just here to find clothes.

Rifling through a bunch of miniskirts, and skimpy tops and dresses, I begin to wonder if my sister owns anything with fabric below the boobs and butt.

I can't see anything I'd wear around the house, let alone on stage in front of a packed house. Her less-is-more style is not for me.

So much stuff is crammed in this room. Even the posters we plastered on the walls as teenagers are still here.

My gaze focuses on the collage hanging over her dresser. It's filled with photos of her and me at various stages of life. I smile at the more recent images of Summer, Christina, and Mom.

I missed so much of Summer's life…and Christina being pregnant…and giving birth. Wow, what must that have been like for her?

Clothes. Hm. Perhaps the lower drawers will reveal something. So far, I've only looked through her underwear drawer, out of desperation.

As I bend down, I spot a pink envelope on the floor. It's got my name on it, in Christina's handwriting.

What's it doing here? I guess it fell off the dresser, or perhaps Summer was playing with it. What in the hell is it going to say?

I'm not sure I even want to open it. Just more of Christina making excuses, and attacking me for not being daring enough with my life.

I sigh, sit on the edge of her bed, and rip open the envelope. I guess I should read it in case it's about Summer.

If she was really studying nursing, it would be amazing. I'm still not totally sure that's actually happening. Not like she hasn't lied before to get me to do shit for her, or lend her money.

But Mom said she hasn't touched a drink, or anything else, since she became pregnant.

Would have loved to have gotten one phone call saying *I don't need bail money, or any money. Let's just be sisters again.*

Nope. Never the good stuff.

I unfold the letter.

Hi Zoe

Sorry for leaving so suddenly, and for not telling you about Summer. Sorry for lying about Mom dying...I just needed to get you here to see I've changed, and to help me get my nursing career started.

I need you to give me this chance, and I hope you'll see I've changed a lot.

How can I see she's changed if she isn't here? Sounds like she expected to have some time before leaving. Maybe she didn't plan to steal everything I own. But her crazy impulses got the better of her. Nothing new there.

I always feel so inferior to you. You're always right. You never get anything wrong. You've always been the favorite, and I get that. I've always been such a failure.

Wait, what? I'm the favorite?! Surely she doesn't believe that! How could she? Fuck. She's the one Mom always defends.

I just want to feel like I'm worth something. I need to do something for Summer. I can't just keep working at the bar, being extra friendly for tips. And then there's Summer's college fund to save for.

I know how you hate me and that's my fault. I know I've always been such a needy bitch to you. I just never knew how to switch it off. I wanted the attention you got, but I wanted to be me, not you. I want to prove to you that I can be different. Prove it to myself.

But I see now, that I can't do this without you. There is no reason in the world for you to forgive me, except that you might want to one day.

I love Summer with all my heart and I want her to have a happy family. I want you to be a role model for her.

I wanted to tell you this so many times, but I just couldn't. Getting pregnant was careless of me. But it is the best thing that ever happened. Summer makes me so happy.

And I want you to be happy too. I can't let you marry when you aren't in love. I know you'd stick it out forever, being miserable, because you always do what's right.

I pray you're ready to talk sometime, and maybe we can be a proper family again. I'll try and keep my hot-headed jabs to myself and listen. I promise. As long as you can cut me some slack and listen to me too.

If you're ready to talk, to give me a chance to make things right, then call me. Love you, Sis.

Oh, not arguing went well now, didn't it? I barely got out of the car and she started in on me.

But wow. This is a lot. She's saying sorry, and even admitting she's the problem. Words I never thought I'd hear, or read in this case.

Maybe I needed to listen. Well, I damn well would listen, if ever she had anything decent to say. I lay back on her bed, staring at the ceiling. She actually wrote all that down? All those feelings. She must want us to connect again. And amazingly, the nursing career is true! That's really incredible.

Suddenly, a strange feeling arises. So strange, I can't quite figure it out. God, I think I feel *proud* of her…she carried and gave birth to Summer, with only Mom for support. And she's been taking care of both of them ever since.

And now she's run away, not to hook up with some loser, or to escape everything. She's actually studying nursing.

Plus, she was right about me marrying George. How did she know how stuck I was? And that I'd be miserable if I went through with it?

It's true. If someone is to marry me, he needs to know me completely. And that includes my family. How could I have been so ashamed of them? I should be ashamed of myself.

I have to call George. God knows what he thinks happened to me. I can't make a future with a past full of guilt and regret. Time to deal with what I did.

Shit! What's the time? I start work in an hour. And still need to lock in an outfit for Saturday.

I yank open the bottom drawer and discover some sweats, blouses, and a pair of black leather pants. Hmm, pretty cool. And they should fit…Christina looked my size when I saw her last…and these sure aren't maternity pants.

I definitely can't spend the night with Jacob tonight. Time to get my shit in order, and move my life forward. Right now, I'm the messed up sister. And guess what? It didn't kill me to admit it.

By the time I'm dressed for work, I feel invigorated. And I actually enjoy the daily walk to the bar. I wave to Mr. and Mrs. Mitchell across the road. Always out in their garden. They used to give us fresh strawberries when we were kids.

Alongside their house, I notice a parked white van. It looks like a utility van. Don't see a logo. Hopefully, there are no cable or Wi-Fi issues in the neighborhood.

I step up my pace and the van starts up. It rolls slowly past me and then roars off. Weird. Now I'm getting the creeps. Goosebumps rise on my arms.

Why would anyone be watching me? Hopefully, it isn't some old friend of Christina's thinking I'm her.

Ignore it. It's nothing at all.

I stride off to work and feel relieved when I arrive at the bar. As if anyone is going to kidnap me in broad daylight, or ever. Still, it made me a little worried and puzzled.

Pushing open the bar door, I spot a familiar figure at the bar.

"Hello, Zoe."

His voice freezes the air in my lungs. My stomach sinks. Crap, it's George. Sitting casually at the bar. I turn back towards the door in confusion. Shit, I can't run back out.

"George." My voice comes out mangled and high-pitched, "what are you doing here?"

"Funny, I was about to ask you the same thing, *darling.*" He snarls.

Darling? Ew, I can feel my stomach sink. I'd never heard George sound threatening before.

"George. I'm sorry. I was going to call. I should have. I'm really, really sorry."

"Damn right you should have called." He moves toward me.

"How did you know where I was?"

"I was worried when you weren't at the church on time. I haven't known you to be late for anything. So, I took the limo to your house, saw you packing your car, and followed you here."

Followed me? Now I'm really creeped out. As I take a step back, I hear Jacob thumping down the stairs.

CHAPTER 10

JACOB

I've finally read George's offer, and its generosity leaves me unsettled. To relieve my gut feeling, I called in a favor at the bureau to do a background check on this guy. Something about him is very *off*. Hopefully, I hear back soon.

It's almost ten. Gotta open the bar. Zoe should be arriving for her shift right about now too.

I notice Zoe standing in the middle of the room. She looks pale, like she's seen a ghost or something. Weird, she usually jumps straight into work.

I follow her gaze to the bar. Oh, George Miller…this is unexpected.

"George, this is a surprise. Everything okay?" I look between him and Zoe. I'm pretty honed at gauging situations, and I sense some tension in the air.

Still, I move forward to shake his hand. *Act normal, don't give anything away.*

"Certainly, Jacob. I think I startled the young lady.

Anyway, I had some time available, so thought I'd take a drive and check the place out. Your chef let me in."

"Right. Well, since you're here George, I'll show you around." I may as well play along.

"Zoe, can you set up the bar ready for opening?"

"Yep."

I don't like the way George smirks as he turns back to Zoe.

"Nice to meet you, Zoe. Thanks for the enlightening conversation."

"Sure." Zoe zips behind the bar, and disappears into the back storage room.

Strange. I didn't even get a smile…even after the last few nights…

"I just read your offer, George. Seems odd to offer this amount of money to manage the bar for six months. What's the catch?"

Still with the smirk. "If I'm buying this place, I need to know it's being run well before I make a decision on my plans for it. I don't like to leave anything to chance."

"Well, sorry to tell you, I don't have an answer to your offer yet. But I'm glad you came by to look around."

I'm somewhat relieved he's still interested. But still, I don't like the rush considering we agreed to talk next week. What's his game?

"I'm sure we have very similar tastes. Tell me what you'd like to see happen with your bar."

Not so sure about similar tastes. But I give him a tour, including the kitchen and storage facilities.

George adds helpful input. He agrees with my ideas to expand the outdoor dining area, revamp the kitchen, and do a complete paint job.

In fact, he's so agreeable, I should've added in an entertainment lounge and swimming pool just for a laugh.

"Can I get you a beer before you go, or something else maybe?" I want him to get to know Zoe a little, and tell him about the live music aspect.

"I have an appointment and need to get back to Ann Arbor soon, but I could do with a scotch on the rocks. Thanks."

We walk to the bar and pull up a stool each. "Hey Zoe, grab me a light beer, and a scotch on the rocks for George, please. Top shelf."

"Sure."

I note George's eyes on Zoe as she prepares our drinks. She looks flushed. I wonder if she's coming down with something.

"Zoe's been testing out live music here recently. It's been going well, definite uptick in profits when she performs. Her country songs have everyone begging for more."

Zoe firmly places our drinks on the bar.

"Country music! *Begging for more.* How about that?" George takes a sip and smiles at Zoe. "You sound very talented, Zoe. How long have you been singing?"

She really looks kind of strained. So shy when it comes to compliments and attention.

"Not very long."

Hm. Obviously, she's not up for conversation today.

But George doesn't look fazed. "Lucky for you, Jacob. It's so hard to find good help these days." He raises his glass to Zoe, who stands there blankly.

"Hard worker, talented, smart. Just like her twin sister, Christina."

"I'm not sure we need to discuss my attributes and

personal life, Jacob." Her voice stings me like a hard slap across the face. Fuck.

"I'll be in the kitchen if you need me."

Well. I screwed that one up. I haven't seen her so edgy since she was asking me for the job.

"Yeah sure. Go ahead." I'm sure I'll hear about that later.

"Twins! Interesting. Will I get to meet Christina?" George grins at me.

"No, sorry. Not today. She's taking some time off. Zoe is filling in for her."

"I see. Not to worry. Maybe we'll meet another time."

"Sure. You might even consider asking Christina and Zoe to manage the place, if I sign. Otherwise, I'm sure you can find someone qualified."

"That could be quite a novelty, twins running the bar," George nods thoughtfully. "And what about you? Got anyone special you're running away with?"

"Nah. I'll be off to get lost somewhere, enjoying the solitude." There he goes again, asking about my personal life.

"Is that right?" Another smirk. This guy needs to learn to smile properly.

"I have a few other possible investment opportunities, so I need a definite answer by Monday."

I sit back and reach out my hand. "That can be arranged. I'll give you a call."

George drains his drink and shakes my hand.

"You do that....oh, and say goodbye to Zoe for me. Tell her I will see her again soon, and we can discuss the future."

"Sure will. You're welcome to come back on Saturday. We're putting on a memorial for Buddy. Zoe is singing all Dad's favorite country songs."

"You know what? I need some downtime. I'll be here."

I watch him leave while I head behind the bar. A couple of tourists come in wanting directions and drinks.

What's Zoe up to back there? As I deliver the drinks to their table, they ask for lunch menus. Bonus.

I buzz the kitchen, tell Willie to be ready for lunch orders, and ask if he can send Zoe back out.

I'm restocking the wine chiller when she appears.

"Jacob. Willie said you want me."

"I want you alright." I ease closer to her, hungry to feel her softness again.

She takes a step back. No smile. How the fuck do you decipher women and their moods? Yesterday she was loving that stuff.

"Alright. Can you watch the bar while I go unpack more stock? I just called Maddie to come in early, since I got stuck showing George around."

"Sure." She's frowning and avoiding eye contact.

"You seem quiet today." *Definitely* on edge about something.

"Just keep me and my family out of bar conversations, ya know?"

"My bad. It wasn't just a customer though. George might become the new owner. By the way, he said it was good to meet you, and he looks forward to discussing the future."

I swear the blood drained out of her face right then.

"Future?" Her voice is quiet. "What does that mean?"

"Like I said, he may buy this place. If we can come to an agreement. Guess you'll work for him if you want to stay on."

She fumbles a glass, and it falls on the counter with a clatter. I hand it back to her.

"That depends on Christina. When she comes back, I won't be here."

"Okay…" Last night she seemed excited about staying on for a while. Something has changed since she left my bed in the early hours.

"You sure you're okay?"

Zoe shakes her head. "Nothing really. A van followed me. Gave me the heebie-jeebies. Well, I thought it followed me, but then it drove off. I'm not sure. Maybe I'm overreacting."

Her eyes are serious, her face still more pale than normal. "A van? Did you get the license plate?" This is the last thing I need to hear. Too suspect for me to ignore. I need to stop fucking around and get back to my plan.

Stop taking Zoe into my bed. What the fuck am I thinking? If this is Brock Barden…her life is in danger. "No more walking home alone, in the dark."

"I'll be heading home after my set from now on. Willie can give me a ride."

Fuck. Well, there it is. Smack right in the face. Problem solved, I guess. Two can play at this.

"Good. I've got this offer to consider. Paperwork to do."

"If you sell to him…George. How soon will that happen?"

"That's the problem. He wants me to stay on and manage for six months. But that's a *hard no* for me. I don't want to stick around here any longer than I have to."

"Don't blame you. Me neither."

"Are you interested in managing the bar?"

Zoe looks like a deer in headlights. "Me?"

"Yeah. You're more than capable." I watch a thousand emotions cross over her face. Hand wringing, a glow of sweat on her brow. I guess that strange van really rattled her.

Damn. I hardly know about her past. I feel the urge to protect her from every prick who's ever messed with her.

"Zoe. I know something is up with you."

"Don't, Jacob. It's nothing I can talk about right now. I'm just worried about Mom and stuff at home." But her rigid face tells me something else, and there's a hollowness to her voice I don't like.

Whatever I'm getting from Zoe right now, isn't the truth. Why does it have to be such a struggle to get the goddamned truth?

Red flag to a bull. And I'm a bull who's stepped through enough piles of shit in my time. I clench my fists in the air in frustration.

"You know what? You're outright lying. And I don't have the time or desire to play cat and mouse. We both have a past. We owe each other nothing. Let's just get back to life before you came into my bar begging for me to-"

"Fuck you, Jacob Grant. You ain't all that. *I begged for it?* You were like a horny dog!"

"Didn't hear you complaining." Why is she even hotter with daggers of anger flashing through her eyes?

"And you won't hear me complain, ever. I work here. Period. What we did was the worst mistake of my life. Sell the bar. I don't care. I'll survive. I'm sure George will be a great boss."

Holy shit! I deserve that and I should apologize. Nope. Cut it off. "Happy for you."

Her lips press together in a thin line. Eyes like slits. "I'll manage the bar till Maddie gets here." She storms away.

All business now, and I know the subject is closed.

And that white van? My nerves are on edge and I feel like punching the wall. I try to call my old boss. Bet he's ghosting me. Sick of my shit over Barden.

Anger and hate swirl inside me. That piece of shit, Brock Barden. He's not even here and he's wrecking my life. The black pit of fear stirs in my stomach. Dammit. Why did Zoe Olsen have to walk into my bar last Sunday night?

My life really can't get any more fucked up.

Or so I stupidly thought…

* * *

An hour later Maddie taps on the office door. Thank fuck, someone to lighten the mood around here.

"Hey Maddie, do you guys need help out front? I'm just finishing the stock update."

"Um, boss…I'm not sure, but…"

"Spit it out Maddie, what's up?'

And then there she is, pushing Maddie aside and rushing at me like a lost, whining puppy dog.

"Baby..!"

The Richter scale of my fucked-up life immediately maxes out.

Bianca. Sobbing dramatically. Makeup running down her distorted face. This day can go eat a bagful of dicks already and it's only lunchtime.

"Please don't tell me to go away, Jacob. There's something you need to know…

"I'm pregnant. You're gonna be a daddy!"

CHAPTER 11

ZOE

I want to burst into tears, but I don't want that big jackass to think he's broken my heart. Like hell. God, this whole thing with George has shaken me up. I know what I did to him may be unforgivable. But what the fuck?

And Jacob acting like that. I can't believe he said I begged him for sex. Arrogant prick! Boy, I really can pick an asshole in a crowd.

"You okay, Zoe?" Willie asks gently. "Perhaps give me that knife and I'll finish prepping the vegetables."

I realize I've been a little harsh on the carrot, and it's certainly not getting served tonight. "Shit, sorry. I was lost in my own world for a bit."

"Yep. Remind me to never go to that particular world with you," Willie grins. "You wanna talk about it?"

"I don't even know where to start."

"I always find if life's doin' a crash and burn, it means you need a change."

"My life has changed so much this week. You've no idea."

"Situations can change, doesn't mean we do."

"Is this one of those *no one can love you till you love yourself* pep talks?"

"You tell me. Here, have a fudge cookie. Works for me every time."

I take the massive sized cookie out to the staff area and pour a coffee. The roast's aroma fills the air. Smells so good.

Willie is right. Time to own up to my shit. Call George. Call Christina. And keep my hands the fuck off of Jacob. Easy.

I crunch into the cookie. There can't be another man on earth to make me feel like Jacob Grant does. But it's just sex. Not real life.

Sex is not love. Love is built on trust and stability. Now I've had my fun. I need to trust my instincts and create my own stability. I don't need a man for that.

Right. No time like now. I pull out my cell and punch in George's number. I've never called him on this phone, but he answers almost immediately.

"George Miller."

"George. It's me."

"Well, well. Zoe. What can I do for you?"

I don't ever remember George being so smug.

"George, I'm sorry. It was an unforgivable thing to do. But there was a family crisis. I had to come back here for my mom's sake. And…well, I should have ended things way before the wedding."

"Zoe. Stop being a brat and come home."

"Excuse me? A *brat*? I'm not your child, George."

"No, but you are my fiancé."

"*Was*."

"You need to come back. We'll explain to everyone what happened. Family crisis you say…?"

"George. The real problem is, I don't want to be married to you. *I can't marry you.*"

"I see." Long pause. "Perhaps I'm not *slumdog* enough for you…like your animal bar owner."

His words are not only shocking but insulting! Besides, how much does he know about my life since I've been in Hillsdale?

"What are you talking about?"

"Come back to the city, and we can discuss our future away from that shithole town."

I've never heard George speak like this. His smugness soon turns cold and calculating.

"I know more than you think I know, Zoe Olsen."

"George, I'm not in love with you. I'm sorry."

"You're a boring bitch anyway…"

Okay, that's enough being nice. "Coming from you? You're the most boring *bitch* I know, George."

His voice lowers dramatically, "I'll ruin your life. Just like you ruined mine. You'll see."

"Better hurry! I'm already fucking it up all by myself, there's nothing left for you to do."

I cut off the call. My heart's racing. Wow. George was always a little obsessive. And it's true, he must have been humiliated by my actions. His anger though…and threats…

What could he actually do to me? Hopefully, now that he's verbally thrown up all over me, he'll let this all go.

But still. I can feel my whole body shaking.

* * *

Jacob barely looked at me all night. Who cares? I've got tips to take home, and I'm much too tired to care about anything else.

As I'm packing my guitar away, I hear footsteps upstairs. I notice Jacob's behind the bar. So, who's upstairs then?

Clipping the guitar case shut, I take a deep breath. After this day, I can't wait to get out of here. Singing relieved my worries for a while, but now the brutal reality of my day is rushing back.

"Hi there!" A petite blonde approaches the stage. Her hair is piled on top of her head with long strands framing her perfectly made-up face. She's wearing a halter neck jumpsuit. It looks like silk. Definitely not your average small-town attire.

Who is she?

"Hey. Loved your set. Awesome voice."

"Thanks."

"I'm Bianca."

"Zoe. Nice to meet you."

Her hard, blue eyes drive into me. What does she want?

"Jacob is my fiancé."

My eyes flick back to the bar. But he's gone.

Fiancé? Didn't he say he's never had a special relationship? Wait…so this is who was upstairs? His *fiancé*?

There must be an explanation. Where has she been this whole time? Please tell me I'm not so stupid to get played.

"We're having a baby."

Holy shit. Time to go.

I can't believe her. But why would she lie? I don't even need the answer to that. Let Jacob deal with it. Not my problem.

"Okay, wow. Congratulations. Sorry, gotta go."

Guitar case in hand, I grab my tips and walk away. I'm on autopilot as I open my locker to collect my things.

I stick my head into the kitchen. Thank goodness, Jacob isn't there. Willie is still working, so I tell him I don't need a lift after all.

I'm far too fragile to wait around. I can't imagine even looking at Jacob right now.

We said *no strings*. But he also lied to me. Then acts like *he* hates lies. So who's the bullshitter now, Jacob Grant?

I get out the door without seeing him. It's a crescent moon and the streets are extra dark. I remember the white van from this morning and pause mid-stride.

Maybe I'm being stupid not waiting for Willie.

Fuck it…I break into a run. It's only ten minutes. Just go.

Finally, Mom's steps are in sight and no one tried to grab me. No van. No strangers. Nothing. Why am I so paranoid?

Mom's sleeping. And Summer is snuggled up in Christina's bed. I kiss her on the forehead, cover her with an extra blanket, and turn on her *Frozen* themed night light she said she got for her birthday.

As I prepare a cup of tea, I search for the number Christina called me from on my wedding day…well, *failed* wedding day.

I sigh, listening to the ringtone, not really expecting her to answer.

"Zoe?" her voice sounds calm.

"Yeah. It's me. Hi." Just don't overreact if she says anything stupid. Take the high road.

"I assumed you wouldn't call."

"I assumed you wouldn't answer."

"Yeah. Well, I guess we always get off on the wrong foot. Sorry for leaving like that. It's just…when you sped away the first time, I didn't think you'd come back. And I couldn't face saying goodbye to Summer all over again."

"Are you ok?" I'm not used to her apologizing.

"Yes. *No*. I guess so…I hope, well, I *know* things are going ok there. Summer told me."

"We're managing. Probably, we're both to blame for the other night. But where are you? What's going on?"

"I don't know, Zoe. Maybe this is a major mistake. Maybe I don't have what it takes to be a nurse."

"Sure you do." But I wonder if she does. "Why nursing anyway? I had no idea you ever wanted to be a nurse."

She sighs. "I guess I finally wanted to do something useful. And when I gave birth to Summer, I really connected with some of the nurses in the maternity ward. After Mom's accident, I often had to go to the hospital with her. Nurses are way better than any doctor at making you feel safe and informed."

"You know you could've told me you were pregnant." I had to say it. Because I'm hurt she didn't tell me. And this is the most rational conversation we've had in years.

"I should have. But I thought you'd be angry at me for being irresponsible again."

"Serious?" I can't say she's wrong, that is how I would have reacted. But now I can't imagine life without our precious Summer.

"And your letter…Do you really think I'm so perfect? That's crazy. Shit, if you had seen what went down today… well, I bet you would've handled everything much better than I did."

"I doubt it. I've spent most of the day crying because I miss Summer. And becoming a nurse means a lot of time away from her. I don't think I can do it. Plus, I really can't afford city rent. Everything is so expensive."

"There must be other options…Maybe you can do some of the courses online?"

"I can't even turn a computer on. I'm such a tech dumbass."

I had to laugh. Mom already mentioned Christina only manages calls and texts on her smartphone. She's actually pretty brave to take on nursing school while learning computer skills on the fly.

"Pretty sure if you can use a smartphone, you can work out any computer. Maybe that's where you start. I can show you."

"Except you'll head straight back to the city." Her voice sounds defeated.

"Actually…maybe not right away. I've been performing at the bar…singing."

"What? Wow! That's amazing."

"Yeah, had to. Apparently, my flirting skills suck, and I need to get tips somehow."

"I'm surprised Jacob is into that. He's been so indifferent about the bar lately. He barely even keeps the place open on Sundays anymore."

"He's cool with it. We have an…understanding. He knows I'm not you, and I need the tips, so he…um…helps me out. He's nice enough. Nothing special. Ordinary, nice guy."

"Holy shit! You did it with him? Zoe!" she squeals down the phone. "He's sex on legs, and I'm pretty sure he has three. Seriously? Who are you and what have you done with my sister?"

How the heck did she know? I swear she has a radar for hookups. "Ok…yeah. It's nothing. Just a one-off thing."

"The hell it is. He hasn't let a woman within a bull's roar of him since he got there. Believe me, we've all tried. There's no way he's packing that heat missile back up after one night." Christina hoots and whistles.

"Cut it out, Sis." This conversation with her is actually fun.

"Listen, not only was it a mistake with Jacob, this whole day totally blew up in my face." Now I'm babbling. But it's a relief to talk to someone about it.

"Why? What happened?" She actually sounds concerned.

"Well, first an unmarked van followed me to work, then Jacob and I argued to the point we're now barely looking at each other. Then…George turned up…saying he followed me here on Sunday…and now he's buying the bar."

"You're kidding!"

"Wait, I'm not even done…Then, Jacob's *fiancé* walks up to me, and tells me straight to my face that she's pregnant with *his* child."

"Are you serious?"

"Totally. And, despite it all, what really gets me is Jacob. What a total dick!"

"Fuck. Back it up a bit. Who was in the van?"

"Out of all that, that's the thing you want to ask about? I don't know who was in the van. It's made me a little paranoid though."

"That's quite a list, huh? Jacob's pregnant fiancé? Strange van? Your ex, *George*, showing up like that, tells you he followed you, and buying the bar? Seems suspicious, doesn't it?"

"Suspicious?"

"C'mon Sis. You can't take everything at face value. George is a dick. Yes? So, let's start there."

"What do you mean?"

"I wouldn't put it past that sleazy ass to hire an investigator on Jacob. He must have seen you two together. Then found out about Bianca and played Jacob to control the situation or cause trouble. It's all a setup so he can get you back. Duh."

"That's insane. This isn't the movies."

"There's no way all that happens in one day. Just too convenient. Here's something I do know about Jacob. Well, two things…"

"You're a natural snoop."

"Shush. First thing is Jacob's ex left him at the altar. He'd never go back to her after that debacle. The other thing is this was many months ago. Did she look pregnant to you? Did you see any bump? That woman has lied so many times to him, he wouldn't trust anything she says."

"How do you know all this about Bianca?"

"He was drunk one night. I helped him upstairs and he dribbled a lot of nonsense about her lying all the time."

"Helped him upstairs? You don't mean?" Don't tell me that. I couldn't handle it.

"No. Never. We're friends, we have a lot of fun. He's just not into me."

"Okay." Phew. I can't handle any more surprises today.

"Listen, maybe I'll come home for the weekend. I'm missing Summer."

"Well, we could use some help at the bar this Saturday. We're doing a tribute to Buddy. I'll be singing his favorite country songs. I'm sure Jacob would be glad to see you."

"The fuck I'm missing that."

"I don't want any arguments though…"

"We'll be okay. But you should talk to Jacob. If George tells him you ran out on your wedding day…just like Jacob's fiancé…well, it might be best to get that news to him first."

"Not like we're getting together. Why should he care?"

"This is the thing with you Zoe, you always think the ones

who care about you the most, don't care. If he's had sex with you, that's *something*. Trust me. He cares. Even if he's denying it. The real question is, do you care? If you do, don't ignore how you feel."

"I'm not going to make a fool of myself."

"Better you be the fool than someone else doing it for you. Like George."

CHAPTER 12

JACOB

"Bianca, I asked you *not* to go downstairs."

I probably shouldn't have let her stay in my room. But if she is pregnant, I can't very well throw her out on the street. Not that the baby is mine. Besides, she didn't even look pregnant.

Besides, I never, ever risked that. Even with my crazy urgency for Zoe, I still have protection on.

"I was hungry." She pouts and sits on my bed.

"Really?"

"Yes. And you can't pretend I don't exist."

Zoe left on her own, despite agreeing to get a ride with Willie. Now all I can think of is if she got home okay. At least I don't have to explain to her why there's a woman in my room.

"I met Zoe. She's a good singer."

Scratch that.

"What did you say to her?" Pressure builds in my veins. This is too much.

"I just told her the truth."

"Fuck, Bianca....What *truth*? Not only do you not know anything about the truth, but you know we'll never be together again. Why have you come back to haunt me?"

She looks down and starts to twirl her bracelet. "I'm sorry. Can't we just try again? For the baby?"

I breathe deeply and look at the ceiling. "You know, it's been months since we last had sex. Besides, I always took precautions."

"Maybe the condom failed."

"I would know."

"Maybe I put a pinprick in it."

Holy Mother of..."Why would you? You don't even like children."

She drops her head...and the tears come again. Real tears. I almost feel sorry for her. I force my voice to sound gentle.

"Bianca. I know you. I know when you're lying. I just want to know why?"

"I'm tired."

I shake my head in resignation. I'm fucking tired too. Sick and tired of my fucked-up life.

"Just sleep here. I'll go elsewhere."

"You can –"

"No. I can't. You can stay tonight but you have to leave tomorrow. If you really *are* pregnant, you know I'm not the father. I just hope your guilty conscience eventually tells me the *real* truth before you go. Then, I expect you to once and for all get out of my life."

I smash out the door and down the stairs. All I can think of is Zoe thinking I have a pregnant fiancé in my bedroom. This day is absolutely wrecked. Like a perfect storm. Hell, do I call her? It's midnight.

Wait. I don't even have her number in my phone...

I go to the office and check the employee records. Hopefully it's the right number. I look around the staff area and see that beat up sofa, shit, I wish I had my hammock here.

With a little luck, Zoe will answer my text, and I can get some sleep.

I lock the door and go to the staff locker room. I flop down on the old, stained couch. Shit, this thing should be thrown out.

Hi Zoe? It's Jacob. U get home ok?

I wait a beat. Nothing. Okay fine. I grab a blanket and pillow from storage. Comes in handy if someone had a few too many drinks, and needed to sleep it off. I walk back to the couch and wearily eye its lumpy form. My phone beeps.

Yes.

Great. She's safe. With that brief answer, it doesn't seem like she'll talk to me. Things got pretty crazy today. I'd at least like to explain about Bianca.

I shouldn't care at all about what Zoe thinks, but I do. I care more about what she thinks I think of her…Having a so-called pregnant fiancé in my room, right after nights of uncontrollable passion, doesn't send the greatest message.

I could never do that to anyone, let alone Zoe.

Can I call?

Another few minutes pause.

Ok.

I connect the call. "Hey."

"Hey." Her voice sounds as smooth as silk.

"I'm sorry about the way I acted before."

"Same."

It's a start. "Look, I hear you met Bianca…"

"Yes. You don't have to explain."

"Yeah, I do. Look, without getting into the gory details, we used to be engaged. She left me. Now she's back saying I'm the father of her baby."

"Okay."

"No. It's not. I mean, I'm *not* the father. Even if she really is pregnant. Shit, even if I was the father, I'm never getting back with her."

"Right."

I sound like a jerk. Making excuses. Her one-word answers aren't helping either.

"Honestly Zoe. There's nothing between Bianca and me. Hasn't been for months. I don't know what game she's playing, but I'll try to get the truth in the morning."

"Maybe she's just pregnant and scared."

"Maybe. If she is, I'll want a DNA test."

"Okay. Look Jacob, as long as we're confessing. I have something to tell you."

"You have a pregnant fiancé too?" Way too soon for jokes. Cool move.

No reaction. I can feel her nervous hesitation. "I do…did have a fiancé."

"You mentioned being engaged."

"Yes, but I have to tell you. My ex, it's George…"

Wait…"*George? George Miller*? As in buying my bar, George?"

"Yes." I could feel her waiting for my reaction on the other end of the call.

George was her fiancé…let me process this a little. "How long ago? I mean, is it an old relationship?"

"Not exactly. As of last Sunday morning."

Well, of all the… "You mean the day you came to Hillsdale? *That day*? You were still engaged to him?"

"Yes. That was the day we were supposed to get married."

I can barely take this information in. Is she saying what I think she is?

"Christina called me that morning. She said Mom was dying. That she had just days to live. I should have gone to the church, but instead, I came here."

"Shit. And today he turns up? He must be pissed."

"Anyway, I thought you should know. With the deal and everything."

"This is crazy. Are you alright? Do you need some time off work?"

"Just the day…I'll still work tomorrow evening, try for some tips. Christina is coming home Saturday. I'd like to make things nice for her and Summer."

"Of course. Just come in when you're ready."

"Okay, thanks, Jacob." She sounds worn out. I know how she feels.

"Get some sleep, see you tomorrow."

I can't believe it. Here I am hating on any woman who would leave someone standing at the altar. But the thought of her marrying *that guy*...

As if he could ever satisfy a woman like Zoe. He probably wouldn't care if he did or didn't.

That fucking snake. If George likes surprise visits so much, well…might have to pay him one myself.

One thing I learned from being a Navy SEAL, if something seemed too easy, it was usually a setup.

Years of special reconnaissance and surveillance

missions, deep in enemy territory honed my bullshit radar to a razor's edge.

Bounty hunting was the same deal. The people I went after were no petty criminals. I worked under the Joint Special Operations Command.

We hunted criminals of the highest intelligence for war crimes, global cybercrimes, and the dark web. Average citizens have no idea what goes on at that level.

We stopped some of the most dangerous people and organizations in the world. Never felt pride, just doing my duty for my country.

Now I can never turn off that side of myself. The nightmares don't help. I just can't seem to let it go. Especially Barden.

How many times he's been thought dead, but then he turns up again with his trail of destruction.

It's many years later, but if anyone's capable of playing the long game, it's him. He gets satisfaction by bringing pain into the world of those he hates. Namely me. He's clever and has enough power and stealth to stay under the radar.

I believe he's still out there, and it's going to take something major to prove to me he isn't.

Slimy George is small fry compared to Bardon. The bad news is…He's not buying the bar. And without that sale, I'll have to find another buyer fast, or just close it down. But that's a lot more hassle. I'd sooner pass it on cleanly and get out.

The urge for sleep slips away. I return to the office to dial up my sources about Zoe's surprise ex. I'll make sure he never bothers her again.

I should hate her for ditching him like that. I know how much it hurts. But now I know that slimeball, I can't blame her. In fact, I would've dragged her out of that church myself.

* * *

Lucky, I know how to tap into a power nap 'cause that couch ain't my friend. I heave myself up. Just past six o'clock.

A hot shower will feel great. I go upstairs and tap on the door. It's slightly ajar.

No answer, so I push it open. "Bianca, you awake?"

Bed's empty. Bathroom too. I see a note on my bedside table.

Jacob.

I'm sorry. I really am.

I'm not pregnant.

George Miller paid me 10k to get between you and Zoe. I really need the money to get myself through rehab. I'm sorry for hurting you. It wasn't fair.

Also, I heard George has men following Zoe. Please don't tell George I told you anything. Because I really need the money. I know you don't owe me any favors but I'm asking you to keep this between us.

Bianca.

That bastard.

Well, this gets resolved today. After my bureau inquiries last night, I know all I need to know about George Miller.

And, maybe there's hope for Bianca yet. I hope she can get her life in order.

* * *

Felicity's mouth literally drops open when she sees me in the doorway. No sports jacket this time. Just a t-shirt, jeans, and my deadly serious *don't fuck with me* face.

I nod toward his office door. She stiffens and slowly nods back. The bastard is in there alright.

Striding across the room, I shove the door open and charge in.

George looks up at me. The phone he's gripping clatters onto the desk. His eyes widen…and as I approach, they keep widening until they're almost popping out of their sockets.

I walk around his desk, grab him firmly by the throat, and lift him clean out of his seat. Then I shove his flailing body against the nearest wall.

"Uh, uh, uh…" He turns red and makes a weird sound. I hope he doesn't piss himself. That'd be disgusting.

"Listen up fuckhead. I know all about your fake shell companies, your money laundering, and your miniature manhood. And I know the authorities are already on your tail, you disgusting, stupid, prick."

He's wriggling like the worm he is, his feet scraping the wall, trying to get traction.

I let go and he thumps on the ground. He clutches his throat as his feet scramble, trying to get away from me. I turn away and look out at the view.

I give him a couple of minutes to comprehend what's happening. I don't want any confusion.

"Pull yourself together. I need you to understand this."

He's cowering. I squat down to his level and look directly into his pale, terrified eyes. His breathing is rapid and sharp, his face pasty white.

"If you ever think about going anywhere near Zoe or her

family again…If you contact her…If you dare even to speak her name, I will take the comprehensive folder of information I have on your illegal activities, stick a fucking bow on it, and send it to the IRS for Christmas.

"And that's not all. If I am reminded of your pathetic existence for any reason, if I ever see you in my town again, or hear you have been near Zoe…. or if you ever mess with Bianca again, I will find you and rip you apart.

"*Do YOU understand*?"

"Yes, yes, yes…I understand!"

Fuck, I think he did piss himself.

CHAPTER 13

ZOE

My head is churning after speaking with Christina. Could all this drama really be because of George? Maybe Bianca *is* pregnant? It's possible.

And if George really is wanting revenge, then how do I get him to leave me alone?

I needed to chill out today. I'm a little anxious about seeing Christina and worried about George…

Not to mention, I can't get Jacob out of my head.

It's good to be with Summer. She is so excited about Christina coming home, she couldn't even eat her lunch. As I get ready for work, she shows me the *Welcome Home Mommy* sign she's making. I give her a big hug and remind myself I need to forgive Christina for her sake. No matter what it takes.

I hitch a ride to work with Maddie. She's the perfect person to get my mind off everything. She soon has me giggling as she describes her roommate from hell, who almost started a fire by shoving a whole pizza box in the oven.

But as soon as we arrive at work, the thought of seeing Jacob sends me back into misery. There's no way I can be intimate with him again after the shock of Bianca's news. And what must he think of me, now I've told him about George?

I have no idea what my future holds. If Christina comes back for good, where does that leave me? *No more job at the bar*, is where. I guess I could try to find accounting work. I definitely can't bear the thought of being in the same city as George.

Performing again has really fired my soul. I don't want to give that up. I don't think I can without destroying something inside of me permanently. Once again, my life is full of *what ifs*.

In less than a week, my world has turned upside-down. It couldn't be more different.

Now that my forgiveness is settling in, I'm actually surprised how much I'm looking forward to seeing my sister.

Having a niece I never knew about has brought me so much joy. Now I can't imagine not seeing her every day, and watching her grow up.

Suddenly, it dawns on me how much I love being with my family. Why did I ever think life is better in the city?

Would I ever meet someone and have kids of my own? A week ago, kids were nowhere on my radar. Now, I can understand what it means to love a child, and the huge responsibility that's involved.

And I imagine all the pain my selfish attitude must have brought Mom over the past few years. I've sure done a shit job at making the right choices.

* * *

I instinctively begin playing an old favorite, *Afraid to Love Again.* As my index finger drops from *C* to the *G* chord, my emotions plummet too. Too late…The lyrics form in my head and I sing the words with more insight than ever before.

If every time that you got hurt, left a scar
And if every dream you ever had, broke your heart
If every time you made a plan, the world came to an end
Then you'd know why I'm afraid, to love again

My voice cracks slightly, and I work hard to keep it together. Damn. I try to hold back the tears, and not let everyone in the bar witness my anguish. As soon as I get through the song, I call a break. I could do with a shot. Just one to dull my senses a little.

"Buy you a drink?"

She looks familiar. Cropped black hair and bright blue eyes.

"Angel- remember me?" She smiles widely, and suddenly memories of my school friend rush through my head.

"Angel! I would never have recognized you!" Her look is a long way from the blonde ponytail, and braces I remember.

"Lucky, I can't miss you, Zoe. Great to hear your voice again after all this time. I'm just in town visiting my parents. They told me you're playing here- my dad's a big fan."

"Really? That's nice of you to say…Actually, I haven't been singing much. I just started these gigs recently."

"Is that right? I'm surprised, you sound so well-rehearsed. Actually Zoe, I wondered what happened to you after you left town. I thought you were pursuing a music career? Weren't you writing your own material there for a while?"

"Oh…well, I got burned by someone in the industry.

Kinda put an end to it all." I catch Maddie's eye and point to the bottle of Jack Daniels.

"I'm sorry to hear that, Zoe," Angel sympathizes, "it's an all too common story."

"Yeah, I guess."

"No, seriously, it *is* Zoe. I'm in the music industry and hear terrible stories about young performers getting screwed over. But you know, it's never too late."

Maddie places down two shots, accompanied by her signature, sunny smile.

Angel raises her glass, and we down the liquor together.

"Great to see you, Zoe. Here," she whips out a business card from her cell case, "I've gotta go, but if you're ever in Nashville, give me a buzz."

"Nashville! It's my dream to get there one day."

Angel gives me a wink, drops some cash on the bar, and heads for the door. I look down at her business card with a sense of awe.

Angel Cox
Executive Assistant
Aurora Group Entertainment
Nashville, TN (615) 555-5268

Well, if I ever get to Nashville, I'll buy Angel a drink. But I doubt that'll be anytime this decade.

* * *

I finally finish my last set. And I feel satisfied that I'm warmed up for tomorrow night.

As I was performing, my gaze kept returning to a poster advertising Buddy's tribute night. He was such a nice man. I take a closer look, and smile at the image of him in his cowboy hat. Then I notice a ticket price and tagline.

Purchase tickets at the door.

All profits to be donated to Youth Village Foster Care.

Well, that's wonderful, but what profits exactly? Who's gonna *pay* to hear me sing? What is he thinking? And where the hell is he anyway?

I haven't seen him all night. Maybe he's with Bianca?

I pack my guitar away and go to help Maddie close down the bar. I'm itching to ask if she knows anything about Jacob's whereabouts.

Finally, after we've cleared the last tables, I walk out of the kitchen and smack, bang into his broad chest.

"Hey, slow down." He encircles each of my upper arms with his big hands and steadies me.

"Oh, Jacob…you're back." The warmth of his hands penetrates my skin.

"Yeah, and I need to talk with you."

"I need to talk to you too…what's up with charging people to come tomorrow night? Do you really think that's a good idea?"

"Fuck yeah, of course they'll pay. All the locals know Buddy did a lot for foster kids. Buddy would have wanted it this way. Besides, great music, complimentary snacks, drink specials…what's not to like?"

"Hm. I don't know…"

"How did tonight go?"

"Another good crowd, nice tips."

"See! They love you, Zoe. You're magic up there. I'm not sure you realize."

"I hope you're right about tomorrow."

"Of course I am…Hey, we really need to talk. Can you meet me upstairs in ten?"

I look at him…upstairs? Shit.

"Don't worry, I can give you a lift home straight after we talk."

I nod. Better to clear the air. And we have a lot to prepare for tomorrow. Everything has to be perfect, especially now I know there's a cover charge involved.

I go to find Maddie. She's so efficient, she's already cleaned the bar, and is tallying the day's revenue.

"Amazing. I've never seen this much money generated in a few hours here. They love you, Zoe."

"Oh, it's not all because of me."

"Well, don't think they're hanging around to see me. But, girl, your talent is being wasted here. You should be in the bright lights. You're so awesome."

"Been there, tried that. It didn't work out."

"What! How?"

"Long story, involving nineteen-year-old me, and a music producer conman."

"Ohh, shit! That sucks. But still, we live and learn. Not too late to try again."

Somehow, I'm not yet convinced to try again.

"Hey Zoe, I'm about done. We can get out of here."

"Okay, well…actually, I'm heading upstairs. Jacob has some stuff to discuss, and he'll take me home."

Maddie smiles, "*...stuff to discuss?* That's what you're calling it now?"

"Stop it. This is business."

"Hell yeah, it is. Hot and dirty business." Maddie wiggles her hips.

I roll my eyes. No hope. "It's about keeping this place open. There was a buyer, but he needs a manager, and Jacob isn't interested. Not sure what's going to happen now. I just hope the place doesn't have to shut down."

"Shut down?! Over my dead body."

"Jacob isn't staying. Who here can afford to buy the place? Doubt he can give it away for free."

"If Christina was back, Willie can chip in, we could run it. With you performing…and maybe we could find some other bands. Or host amateur nights..."

"Except Christina needs time to do her nursing studies. And I'm not sure I can commit long term."

"Christina also needs money. She can build some savings, and then work out how she does her training. I'll ask her tomorrow. Can't wait to see her. I really miss her fun personality…No offense."

"None taken. I think I agree with you."

As I go to meet Jacob, I wonder if Maddie's idea is an option…Would Christina be reliable enough to help manage a bar?

I tap lightly on his door. No answer. I knock a bit harder.

"Just a second," he yells.

I stand there another minute before the door opens. And there he is standing like some *Adonis*. Towel around his waist. Wet hair tousled. A few droplets of water clinging to his skin. I fight the urge to lick them off. Lord help me please. This isn't going to be easy.

"Oh sorry. I needed a shower and thought I had more time. Come in."

I walk past him. He smells incredibly edible. Gah! Get dressed, get dressed, get dressed.

"I'll just get dressed. Not like it's anything you haven't seen before."

Hmm, thanks for pointing that out. Not helpful. The aroma of him, this intimate space. My senses are in hyper-mode, taking in every detail.

I notice sealed boxes in the corner. A sharp pang of

impending loss radiates as I think about him leaving. In fact, looking around, it's almost like he's already gone because it may as well be a hotel room for all the personal effects on show. No photos, no piles of books, no mementos.

And what will I be to him after he leaves? Just a blurred memory, that fades further into oblivion each day he's gone.

CHAPTER 14

JACOB

I pull on some briefs, jeans, and a t-shirt. She said no more sex. So, I will respect her boundaries. Going without sex never bothered me. Going without sex with Zoe next to me is proving a lot more difficult.

The bar is still mine as of today and I have zero clue what my plan is, but one thing I do know. I'm leaving. I have no choice until I know Brock Barden is really dead.

"I'm not selling to George." I blurt out as I exit the bathroom, "and, so you know, the van following you… it was his guys."

Her hands fly to her face, and she shakes her head in disbelief. "Are you sure?"

"Yes. Plus, he bribed Bianca to lie to me. She's had problems and needs money. He paid her to cause trouble. He tried everything to get you to go back to him, to save face."

"I made it perfectly clear that was never happening. God, I can't believe he is so evil."

"There's more. George is in serious shit with his rogue

financial activities. He's about to realize he has a lot more to lose than an ex-fiancé. His business partners will be piling on serious heat right about now because the IRS is sniffing around."

Her eyes widen. "Are you serious? He's caught up in illegal activities? How do you know all this?"

"Let's just say, I know a few people of influence. And after our conversation today, he'll never bother you again. That's a guarantee."

"Oh, Jacob, I'm sorry you had to get involved in my personal life. But thank you. That's a huge relief. God, I had no idea what kind of man he was."

"Here's a suggestion. Next time you commit to marrying someone, do a background check."

She shakes her head, and raises her palm like she's making a pledge. "Nope. Not happening. Forget marriage. Definitely not worth the risk."

I laugh. "Can't say I disagree."

Her face turns serious again. "So, you really think he won't be back? That he'll leave me alone?"

I want to pull her to me and tell her what I'd do to protect her. That I would lay my life down for her. *Can't right now. There's still the risk with Barden.*

"He won't come near you again. I made things very clear."

We stare at each other. This is going south very quickly if I don't say something.

"Okay, back to business. About tomorrow night. Let me grab my list."

I get my notes together and drop onto the seat next to her. Too close. I want to reach out and touch her upturned face. Kiss her throat.

"Here's what we discussed. All of Dad's favorite songs

and artists. Which ones do you want to perform? Do you want to do any of your original stuff?"

She takes the page and scans it, nodding. "Yes, I know most of these."

"By the way, Zoe, I've been checking into local talent. There are a few options, so looking ahead, you don't have to perform every night. But if that's what you want, well it's up to you."

I know she needs the money, but I don't want her to burn out trying to be everything for everyone.

"Are you keeping the bar?"

I swear I saw a little hope in her eyes. Maybe that's wishful thinking.

"No, I really can't, unfortunately. I'm moving up north as soon as possible."

Her eyes narrow, but she looks away before I can read her emotions.

"Jacob, I've been talking with Maddie. She thinks she could get Christina to commit for a year or so, maybe Willie can pitch in. Perhaps they could run it?"

Interesting idea. The main thing is to get my name off the place. If Barden tracks it to me, he's likely to burn it to the ground, with everyone inside.

"Jacob?"

"Yep, yep. Sorry just thinking a million things."

"You look worried."

"No, that's good news. I'll talk to Maddie. Maybe there is a solution to keep the bar open."

"You're in a hurry to get out of Hillsdale, then?"

"It's complicated. But yeah." I can't even explain to her what it's all about. Do *I* even know what it's about?

What I *do* know is there are only four from my squadron still alive. I'd trust my life with. Two of them are still on active duty. The others are probably trying to live a normal life like me. Fat chance.

After what we'd seen and done, normal doesn't calculate.

Zoe's thumb presses across my brow, and I realize how hard I'm frowning. Her touch both soothes and arouses me.

"I'll miss you. I know it's only been a few days, but I think we're friends."

Her green eyes capture mine. The soft falter in her voice makes my heart lurch.

"Friends my ass. I don't kiss my friends the way I kiss you." My voice is husky too. Fuck, I try, but Zoe just speaks to my primal needs.

Her eyes flicker. "I think I've forgotten how you kiss me."

That's it. I reach for her and our heat collides, I crush my lips to hers.

I want to be gentler. It's impossible. She groans beneath me, not holding back. I'm already rock hard, and curse my restrictive jeans. The kiss seems to go on forever. I'm not complaining, though my nuts are.

We break apart, panting in each other's arms.

"We did say *no strings*." Her voice is breathy and sexy as fuck. "I know you're leaving. Heaven knows what I'm doing. I still want to do this."

"Same here." I get up and take her hand.

We move to the bed, she sits and reaches to unbutton my jeans, and lowers the zipper. Her lips follow her hands up my chest to meet my lips.

"Don't tease. I'm not sure I have that much resistance."

"Undress me."

I take my own sweet time removing her clothes until she's in her bra and panties. I can see a glimpse of her hard nipples through the lace. Her generous hourglass figure is breathtaking.

"Zoe. You're so beautiful. I want to spend all night with you."

"You know I have to be home by morning."

"I better get started then."

I search in my bedside drawer for a condom. Shit, do I have any?

"Sorry, what a buzzkill. Just looking for protection."

"Damn! Don't worry, I get it. It would be good if everyone was that responsible. The're enough kids stuck in the foster system."

I stare at her. "Exactly. Did you know foster kids are getting rehomed through ads on the goddamned internet? The whole system is broken."

"Is that why you're donating tomorrow's profits to foster kids?"

Ah! What does it matter if she knows? I should just come clean with her.

"Yeah, I used to be one. A throwaway kid for junkies. Until Buddy adopted me."

"Oh my god, Jacob. I didn't know."

"No way you could."

Okay. This conversation took a serious turn, and is getting way too clinical. Need to find a condom.

Ah, found one! Looks a little ragged, but it will do. Now, I just have to get us back in the mood.

Not gonna take much for me, seeing her arched back against my pillows like that.

"I appreciate you being so careful. A niece is enough for me right now."

"Can we just stop talking? Time is ticking." I take her into my arms again, and I'm not stopping this time. I move her to the center of the bed, and slowly explore her most sensitive parts, through the lacey fabric.

She's twisting, squirming, and groaning beneath my fingers, my mouth. I slip the condom on. I only have this one, so I have to make it count. It will be long and slow until she begs me to give her release.

Mouth, fingers, hard heat. Not necessarily in that order. I have a few hours, and I intend to use up every second making Zoe crazy with desire.

Tonight, she is mine to take completely. I need this moment to last in my memory for a long time. Because once I say a proper goodbye to Dad, I'm out of here.

* * *

As usual, she's gone when I wake.

Somehow, her absence makes everything feel washed out and tasteless. Even my brute-strength morning coffee tastes like dishwater.

Well, may as well get used to it. I'm about to go into hibernation mode for *fuck knows how long*.

There's not much to pack. I'll pick up some essentials on the road.

The main thing is getting the bar contract done. No sale. But Maddie's enthusiasm pushed another idea to mind. I can lease the bar to her, and whoever will partner with her. Christina…or Willie perhaps.

It's a generous offer, with lease payments tied to a small percentage of profits. Because as long as one of them takes over the licenses, I really couldn't give a shit.

I already set up a meeting this morning with my lawyer to draw up the contracts, so I can settle the details remotely… Up till a point.

I've set a hard boundary for when I totally cease communication. That's when I really focus on shutting down any untidy trails.

Perhaps Zoe will change her mind and hang around too. Her accounting skills would be a bonus. Either way, I can't be attached.

This way, at least I can hand over the keys and walk away.

CHAPTER 15

ZOE

What a mess. How frickin hard can it be to make pancakes?

My suitcase is on the floor near the dining table, with its contents spilled out…Christina's bags are strewn nearby. And torn wrapping paper from Summer's gifts is spread across the room.

"Summer, watch out honey!" She nearly bowls me over. Having raided my freshly returned belongings, she's now racing around wearing my silk scarf and straw hat, holding aloft her brand-new *Elsa* doll.

"Zoe, darling, let me help." Mom finally comes to my rescue.

How is it she can mix and pour batter, and cook it perfectly, while I've been scraping up this sticky mess the last twenty minutes? And she's doing it all while literally standing on one leg. Hm.

Christina grabs Summer, now on her third circuit of the kitchen, and lifts her up into a hug. "Mommy, stop squeezing me so hard!" Summer giggles and wriggles her way back down.

"Oh my God, she grew like a beanstalk! What have you been feeding her, human growth powder?" Christina plops onto a stool and picks at the sliced strawberries I've prepared.

"When do I get the hot, juicy details of your raging love life, Sis?"

"Christina!" I roll my eyes Mom's way…God, she can't keep anything to herself.

"Oh, dear. You don't think I notice you sneaking back into the house at five most mornings? I'm certain the bar shuts quite a bit earlier than that." Mom casually flips another restaurant quality pancake.

Christina flashes me a mock shocked look. "Secrets out… may as well spill the hot sauce…" Grabbing a banana from the fruit bowl she holds it aloft in both hands. "Just how big are we talking, Sis?"

I snatch it out of her hands. "Oh my God, you're relentless."

I can only imagine how she's going to behave once we see Jacob at the bar. I could almost laugh about it, except for the gnawing hole in my gut.

As usual, our lovemaking was powerfully intense last night. But there was also a beautiful tenderness that lingers with me. How on earth am I going to say goodbye?

* * *

I notice people milling outside the bar. Shit, are they gonna pay the ticket price Jacob's enforcing or choose to leave?

Christina parks the car and we coordinate efforts to get

Mom on her crutches. Summer dances around us, still clutching *Elsa*.

"Aunt Zoe, are you gonna sing *Let It Go?*'

"I'm not sure Summer, I might need your help with that one."

She beams back. "Maybe…I know all the words."

As we get closer, I see Harriot has been recruited to handle payments at the door.

"Oh, look at you gorgeous ladies! Christina! Wait right there so I can give you a big hug." Harriot adjusts her glasses and smiles up at the group of seemingly happy, paying customers.

"Folks, go on through, enjoy!"

We follow them inside, and I pause, soaking up the scene.

It's incredible. The bar is lined with people, and I can hardly spot an empty table. I watch as Christina enters the fray, and gets swept up in greetings and hugs from various locals.

She also attracts many other eyes, and I admit, she really knows how to work a simple singlet top, cut-off denims, and cowboy boots. My silk scarf wrapped casually around her neck highlights her eyes and her bright red, braided hair.

Happily, we called a truce on the clothing wars, because Christina's black leather pants fit me like a glove. And paired with my expensive jade-colored blouse, I finally feel like I might look the part of a performer.

As I assist Mom through the crowd, I try to keep Summer close, but suddenly she disappears toward the bar.

"Hey, Summer this way!" I'm about to run after her when I hear her delighted laughter.

Jacob emerges with her astride his big shoulders, her little hands gripping his forehead, her doll wedged in the crook of his arm.

"Jacob…take me to Willie's cookie jar!" Summer commands.

"Well, you heard the little lady- we'll be back soon!" Jacob smiles broadly and moves back through the crowd. He ducks and weaves his head slightly, and is rewarded with more of Summer's giggles.

I smile as they retreat. Then, I turn and meet Mom's waiting eyes. "What?"

"Nothing. Except you look one hundred percent, completely and totally in love, my girl. I hope you know what you're doing."

I laugh. "Come on Mom, let's get you seated." But as much as I want to brush off her observation, I know it's true. My heart is primed for a battering of epic proportions.

As I prepare for my first set, I realize that's why this whole day feels so strange, like being suspended in time. Here I am, in the heavenly position of playing the music I love, while being supported by an appreciative crowd, especially my family.

But the flip side is being frighteningly aware of the approaching hell. And it edges closer with each song, each round of applause, and each sweet look into Jacob's soulful eyes.

* * *

Buddy's tribute was a triumph. As much as Jacob always insists the bar isn't his scene, he certainly knows how to run it.

He planned for the crowd, and had sufficient staff, food

and beverages on hand, so even he could step back and enjoy himself.

Maybe a little too much. By the time I was done performing, he was definitely mellow. *Top shelf whiskey* mellow.

Perhaps it was the relief that Maddie and Christina agreed to lease the bar. And likely the emotion of saying the final goodbye to his dad.

As I said good night, with Summer asleep in my arms, we agreed to see each other the next day. But it never happened. He left before the bar even opened.

And now I've been without him for three months.

For the first couple of weeks, he called almost every day. Mostly to liaise about the lease. But then he handed everything over to a lawyer to manage.

Somehow, Christina and I are getting along enough to work together. Maybe because Maddie makes a good buffer for any disagreements.

With Mom mobile again, Summer is well cared for on the nights we work late. Thursdays to Sundays are super hectic. Our talent search turned up so many local gems, we have performers lining up for a chance to play.

I should be content. But my spirit is restless. I dream of Jacob. Wondering if he's okay, wherever he is. Wondering if I'll ever see him again.

It's lucky I'm so focused on work. Because I know it's crazy to hold out hope for an absent man.

I do wish things could be different for us. But I also get that he has demons he needs to deal with. Not something I could really help with.

"Hey, Sis, someone was looking for you today. I said you'd be there by happy hour."

"Who?"

"I'm not a psychic, but she gave me this card." Christina

looks like she's about to explode. I can always tell when she has a secret.

"Just show me, then." I scan the card and flip it over to find handwriting on the back. No way!

"This is for real? Angel's inviting me to perform in Nashville?!"

Christina jumps up and down cheering. "Yes! You're gonna be famous!"

Excitement ripples through me, like I've just been handed all my dreams on a platter. I grab Christina's hands. We bound around the room like lunatics.

Then I check the card again…to make sure.

Zoe,

Formally inviting you to perform at our event next month-

Nashville Vocal Talent: Emerging Artists.

It's a big deal. Call me for details asap.

Angel

That exposure has launched hundreds of the biggest country music artists in the U.S. Suddenly, I feel hot. Incredibly hot. Like I want to faint. Uh oh.

I run for the toilet with my hand over my mouth. Must be all the excitement.

"You okay, Sis?"

I can't answer. All I can do is retch over the toilet bowl. Christina is with me, holding my hair back.

"Shit. Did you eat that chicken that's been in the fridge for days?"

"Only ate a sandwich. No chicken."

"Are you alright for work?"

"I think so."

I did feel much better. Too much emotion is all.

* * *

Angel's at the bar when I arrive. It's a relief we can meet face to face because our phone conversation left me with even more questions.

"Angel, this is serious right? If I say yes, I'm definitely in the show?"

She laughs. "A hundred percent. I don't mess with talent, Zoe. I'll be in town for a couple of days. We'll go over the contracts and details. You can get your lawyer to look over everything."

I guess I could call the lawyer Jacob used for the bar. "Ah, umm. Yep, I sure will."

"I have some lawyer contacts that specialize in the music industry if you like." She grins.

"That might be a good idea."

"Zoe, this is a great chance to get your music out there. You might want to prepare yourself for what's ahead. A lot of attention, and all the pressure that comes with it. But I'm confident we can support you all the way."

"Oh my God, Angel. I honestly don't know what to say."

"Just say yes, and we'll progress from there."

"Yes! Definitely yes! I'll do anything to make the most of this chance, Angel."

"I know you will, Zoe. Take a day to let it sink in. I'll email through all the details. Congratulations."

As soon as Angel leaves, Maddie rushes over.

"I hear you're leaving us for the bright lights."

"Can my sister ever keep a secret?"

"No way. Not from me anyway. But seriously, congratulations, you deserve it!"

"Thanks, Maddie. If it wasn't for you guys, I wouldn't have this amazing opportunity."

"Sure you would. You just had to get your confidence back. And your personal power."

"That is a work in progress." It really is, but I'm so much happier than I ever imagined was possible.

I feel…*authentic.* Like I've finally tapped into who I really am. And what I want in my life. No secrets anymore, my life is an open book.

Except for that closed chapter on Jacob. If I could love a man forever, it would be him. At least, I'd be willing to give it a shot.

"Hey." Maddie breaks into my thoughts. "Some guy was asking about Jacob today. No one I recognized."

"Really? What did you tell him?"

"I just did what Jacob told me to do. I told him *if I never hear from that asshole ever again, it will be too soon*."

"Do you think he believed you?"

Maddie shrugs. "Not sure."

"Maddie, do you think someone is after Jacob? Is that why he had to leave?"

"I really don't know. All I know is the nightmares that man has are epic."

I look at her sharply.

"Oh, no, don't get the wrong idea Zoe. Of course, we didn't…I only know because I could hear him yelling sometimes, when I bunked here a few weeks. On that couch in the staff area…not in his room."

"It's not that. I mean, every time I left, he was sleeping so soundly, he never even knew I left."

"Well maybe he stopped having them. I asked him once,

and he brushed me off. Got a little angry. Said it was nothing, it happened every night, and he was used to it."

"Question is, what would be so bad, that it would make him yell so loud you could hear him down here?"

"Not something I'd ever want to know about."

I go behind the bar, intending to help Maddie with the beer keg. But I can't resist opening a bag of potato chips. Need something salty. Maybe something sweet…There's candy in my bag. That hits the spot. Chips and candy. Perfect combo.

But what if someone is after Jacob? His Navy stint, and bounty hunter days…he must have been in some dangerous situations. He said he had friends in high places, and the level of fitness he maintains is a sign of extreme training.

There is definitely more to Jacob than meets the eye. More than he wanted anyone to know about. I hope he can find peace. At least our nights together were peaceful. I didn't ever witness his nightmares.

Oh, how I wish I could have one more night with him.

CHAPTER 16

JACOB

I didn't make it as far north as I had hoped. But I got a great parcel of fertile land. Just gotta wait for spring.

There's no doubt I left a good chunk of my heart back in Buddy's Bar. But I also know I need to do this to keep her safe.

Barden still dogs my thoughts night and day. But even the threat of him pales against how much I miss Zoe. The warmth of her next to me at night. Her smile, her flashing eyes, her silky skin.

If he comes for me. I'll at least be ready. I have plenty of wood chopped, food reserves and stored weapons. The less time spent traveling to town, the better.

The sound of a stick cracking from behind me. Fuck! I swing around, the axe still in hand. Who or what got past my booby traps?

"You're not such a hard man to find. A bit rusty on the traps, I see."

A tidal wave of relief sweeps through me. “Holy fuck, Chet. I thought someone was here to kill me.”

“Yeah, well, it wouldn’t be hard. Your ass has gone soft.”

Son of a bitch. What a relief to see him.

“Let’s get inside. I have whiskey to warm us up.”

Chet and I worked on many missions together. I know he’s on the level. Also, he’s the one person in the world who knows me well enough to track me down anywhere.

“Can’t say I’m sorry to see your ugly face.”

“Wish I could say the same, but, nope.”

We laugh a bit. Man, if anyone ever *got me*, it’s him.

“Why are you here? Is everything okay?”

“I have some news I thought you’d want to hear.”

“Barden?”

He nods.

“Fuck. He’s alive…I knew it.” The pit of my stomach clenches.

“Nope. He’s definitely not. Proof. DNA proof. From bones found.”

“Barden wouldn’t stop at cutting something off to fake a death.”

Chet shakes his head. “This evidence is definitive. He is one hundred percent officially dead. So, I thought I’d better come save your babyass before you kill yourself out here over winter.”

“I can’t believe it’s true.”

Chet reaches inside his jacket and pulls out papers sealed in plastic. “I guessed as much. Read this. You know damn well I’m not coming to tell you this unless I’m certain.”

That’s true. Chet would never get my hopes up. He knows how much this means to me.

I swallow a shot of whiskey. The empty glass reminds me

of Zoe. That Sunday night, when she turned up in my bar. When I totally fell for her.

Can this intelligence be true? Is there really nothing to hold me back?

"You doin' refills? It's a long stretch outta here for you." Chet interrupts my thoughts.

"What makes you think I'm going anywhere?"

He laughs. "Still shit at poker face, I see."

"Lying about what?"

"That look means you've creamed your jeans over some chick. She must mean a lot to you. Better go see she hasn't forgotten your candy-ass."

"Too much to do here before snow sets in." I know that sounds stupid. But what if I get there and she knocks me back?

"This palace you've got goin' here? I'll take care of it. Come visit me when the snow melts."

"Are you serious?"

"Sure. This here is luxury compared to Kazakhstan. Now fuck off. I need sleep."

I sit to thumb through the report. It's official, courtesy of the Joint Special Operations Command.

Fuck. Here comes my new life. I can't wait, gotta go *right now*. I shove some clothes in my backpack. How far would I get walking at this time of day?

"Take the Polaris you've got hidden out there in the back." Chet mumbles, his eyes still shut.

"You don't miss anything do you?"

"Had good training having to watch your back all the time. Haven't you gone yet?"

"What if you need the Polaris?"

"Hide it somewhere just before you get to the first town.

I'll walk out tomorrow and get it. Shouldn't be hard to find." His sarcasm shines through his words as always.

"You're a funny son of a bitch."

"Stay longer and you'll have to make love to me."

"I'm out. Thanks, Chet, you really are the best buddy anyone could have."

"No one likes a kiss-ass. Now go!"

* * *

Traveling back to Hillsdale brings new emotions. Like the fact that being isolated just suppresses trust in myself and definitely trust in others. I really do miss being around people.

After Zoe entered my world, I really felt happy…despite the anxiety I had about Barden being a threat to my life and others. Now that I know he is dead once and for all, the air is lighter and I truly can be happy.

I know Zoe felt something with me too. The day I left was so difficult for both of us.

Arriving outside Buddy's, a wave of excitement fills me.

I can hear a lively crowd carrying on inside. The sweet sound of her guitar and beautiful voice fills in the air.

I've been contemplating since I left Chet, how do I just walk back in? What do I say to her?

"Finally. I was about to come and hunt you down myself."

"Christina? What are you doing out here?"

"I might ask you the same thing. Why are you back? You better not be here to break my sister's heart."

"What? No...I mean, she might break mine."

Christina strides towards me with a friendly hug.

"Welcome home, Jacob. I hope you got your shit together?"

"Yeah, I believe I have."

"Good. because it won't be easy, ya know."

"What are you talking about?"

"You'll have your big hands full in another six months." Christina smiles with a twinkle in her eye.

"Huh?" Why all this cryptic crap?

"How long have you been gone, Einstein?" She plants her hands on her hips and tilts her head.

"Three months."

"What's three plus six?"

"Um nine…I don't get what you're…"

"*Nine months*."

Holy shit. Wait…what? "You're kidding right?"

"I'm the last person to joke about an unplanned pregnancy."

Her bombshell almost knocks me over. "There's no way. I always use protection. Literally always."

"How fucking old are you? Fourteen? Tell me you don't still believe in Santa Claus too? Put it this way. If the baby isn't yours, that means Zoe was having sex with someone else at the same time as you."

When she put it like that. I know that wasn't happening.

Wait, what about Bianca's threat that she poked holes in one of the condoms? Was she telling the truth about that? Hard to say what was truthful with her.

"Wait, what about George?" My fist clenches.

Christina waggles her pinky finger and rolls her eyes. "Don't worry, she already spilled on the pathetic George scenario…they hadn't done the deed for months before I saved her from marrying that loser."

"Was she going to tell me?"

"If you ever got your ass out of hiding, I guess so. Also, she has no clue yet."

"Fuck. How do you know then?"

"Let's call it twin's intuition. And if I get phantom labor, I'm kicking you in the balls."

I had to laugh at her. "So, I'm going to be a father. Wow."

"Go in there and tell her you love her."

"What if she doesn't love me?"

"Ha. Don't worry. She does."

Once again, Zoe Olsen turns my whole world upside down and she doesn't even know it yet.

"Also, don't tell her I told you. Let her figure it out." Christina walks towards the door.

"How do I..?"

"You'll work it out numb-nuts."

I follow Christina into the bar. It's packed tight with revelers. But the crowd parts as I walk towards the sound of her clear, captivating voice.

I hear Maddie from behind the bar, "Hallelujah, Jacob's back!"

Others call my name, but my tunnel vision focuses on the stage until I see her.

Then I stop, transfixed.

Her red hair, spilling across her pale face, her eyes shut tightly as she hits a high note. It hangs there for an eternity and then cascades with the crowd singing along.

I'm completely lost in her voice. My heart is beating so loudly, it's as if it's part of the music, like it's gonna burst clear out of my chest.

I wait expectantly for her voice to rise to the next note, but abruptly, it falls silent along with the guitar.

Her eyes are on me…those beautiful emerald eyes, staring intently.

She's frozen mid-song. A murmur rises from the crowd.

I gain speed toward the stage. The need to grab her, feel

her, hold her, kiss her consumes my thoughts. As I walk across the dance floor and up to the stage, she doesn't move a muscle, just looks at me blankly.

I take the guitar from her arms, just like that first night we were together. I rest it on the stand next to her. I reach for her hands and gently tug her upwards until she's standing beside me.

Holy shit she is so beautiful. I cup her cheek, rub my thumb over those luscious, kissable lips.

Finally, a sound. "Jacob?" A sob rises from her throat. Her eyes glisten.

I draw her closer, my hand behind her head, fingers wrapped in her silky, long hair. At last, I lean down and press my lips against hers. Stars prick my eyeballs, energy erupts between us. Her hands grip my neck and we meld together.

I'm not even conscious there's an entire room of people surrounding us until the crowd erupts, cheering. But they sound a long way away.

I only know that by some miracle, I'm holding everything I want, need, and care about right here in my arms. And not one soul will ever take her away from me.

* * *

"Nashville! Baby, I always knew you were a super star!" I'm blown away, it's all I can do not burst into the bar and shout her news to everyone.

"You'll come with me?"

"You bet your gorgeous ass I will! Consider me your personal bodyguard." No way I'm letting her go alone. With her looks and talent, in an industry of leeches, she's gonna need my full-time protection. And sure as hell, that's what she'll get.

"Hold that thought!" She runs for the bathroom.

"You okay?"

She bangs the door shut so hard it pops open again. I hear the toilet flush and then she's at the sink splashing water at her face and gargling mouthwash like crazy.

I lean on the doorframe thinking about Christina's comment about Zoe having no clue she is pregnant.

"At first I thought it was something I ate, but now maybe it's nerves for Nashville..."

"Okay, sure…nerves. But the only time I see ladies around here running to vomit is 'cause they drank too much…or are pregnant. What have you been drinking, little lady?"

"How could I be *pregnant* when we used condoms every time? Besides, I didn't think you wanted kids." Christ, how can she not realize what she means to me?

"Zoe, all I know is I want *you*. Anything else that happens after that will only make me wonder even more how I became such a lucky bastard."

She steps into my arms and lays her head against my heart.

"And if I'm not pregnant?"

"Then, we can try again…and again…or maybe we adopt Zoe."

She leans back, looking up into my eyes. A powerful surge of adrenaline hits me.

There is absolutely no doubt in my mind.

"Zoe, I now know real love. And it's *you*."

The End

www.ingramcontent.com/pod-product-compliance
Lightning Source LLC
LaVergne TN
LVHW012117170826
845678LV00014BA/2976

* 9 7 9 8 3 7 4 6 7 0 3 2 5 *